RANDOM
HOUSE
LARGE
PRINT

Shepherds
Abiding

Also by Jan Karon
available from Random House Large Print

IN THIS MOUNTAIN

A COMMON LIFE:
The Wedding Story

THE MITFORD YEARS

JAN KARON

Shepherds Abiding

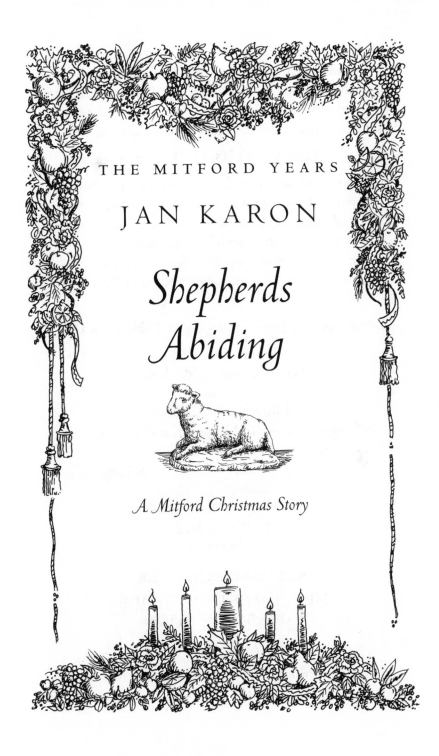

A Mitford Christmas Story

Copyright © 2003 by Jan Karon

All rights reserved under International and Pan-American Copyright Conventions. Published in the United States of America by Random House Large Print in association with Viking, New York, and simultaneously in Canada by Random House of Canada Limited, Toronto. Distributed by Random House, Inc., New York.

Library of Congress Cataloging-in-Publication Data

Karon, Jan, 1937–
Shepherds abiding/Jan Karon.
p. cm.
ISBN 0-375-72827-9
I. Clergy—Fiction.   2. North Carolina—Fiction.
3. Cráches (nativity scenes)—Fiction.   4. Mitford
(N.C. : Imaginary place)—Fiction.   5. Large type
books.   I. Title
PS3561.A678S47 2003
813'.54—dc22
2003058993

www.randomlargeprint.com

FIRST LARGE PRINT TRADE
PAPERBACK EDITION

10   9   8   7   6   5   4   3   2   1

This Large Print Edition published in accord with the standards of the N.A.V.H.

To the honor and glory
of the Child, Emmanuel,
God with Us

Acknowledgments

Warm thanks to:

Family Heirlooms of Blowing Rock, where I found the Nativity figures written about in this story; my daughter, Candace Freeland, who got excited with me and contributed a great idea; Mrs. George (Bobby) Walton, who, without knowing my need, sent a helpful book of Nativity images; my publishers at Viking Penguin, who are ever gracious to Mitford; Fr. James Harris, who is always helpful and tender of spirit; Jefferson Otwell; The Right Reverend Keith L. Ackerman, SSC; Gary Purdy; Hoyt Doak; Lisa Knaack; Sherman Knaack; Mike Thacker; Bill Lapham, Asher Lapham, and Michael Summers.

Special thanks to:

Stefanie Newman, who restored the actual Nativity figures to their present charm and beauty.

*A*nd there were in the same country shepherds abiding in the field, keeping watch over their flock by night.

And lo, the angel of the Lord came upon them, and the glory of the Lord shone round about them; and they were sore afraid.

And the angel said unto them, Fear not: for behold, I bring you good tidings of great joy, which shall be to all people.

For unto you is born this day in the city of David a Saviour, which is Christ the Lord.

And this shall be a sign unto you; Ye shall find the babe wrapped in swaddling clothes, lying in a manger.

And suddenly there was with the angel a multitude of the heavenly host praising God, and saying,

Glory to God in the highest, and on earth peace, good will toward men.

And it came to pass, as the angels were gone away from them into heaven, the shepherds said one to another, Let us now go even unto Bethlehem, and see this thing which is come to pass, which the Lord hath made known unto us.

And they came with haste, and found Mary, and Joseph, and the babe lying in a manger.

And when they had seen it, they made known

abroad the saying which was told them concerning this child.

And all they that heard it wondered at those things which were told them by the shepherds.

Luke 2:8–18, KJV

Contents

One

*T*he rain began punctually at five o'clock, though few were awake to hear it. It was a gentle rain, rather like a summer shower that had escaped the grip of time or season and wandered into Mitford several months late.

By six o'clock, when much of the population of 1,074 was leaving for work in Wesley or Holding or across the Tennessee line, the drops had grown large and heavy, as if weighted with mercury, and those running to their cars or trucks without umbrellas could feel the distinct smack of each drop.

Dashing to a truck outfitted with painter's ladders, someone on Lilac Road shouted "*Yee*haw!," an act that precipitated a spree of barking among the neighborhood dogs.

Here and there, as seemingly random as the appearance of stars at twilight, lamps came on in houses throughout the village, and radio and television voices prophesied that the front passing over the East Coast would be firmly lodged there for two days.

More than a few were fortunate to lie in bed and listen to the rain drumming on the roof, relieved to have no reason to get up until they were plenty good and ready.

Others thanked God for the time that remained to lie in a warm, safe place unmolested by worldly cares, while some began at once to fret about what the day might bring.

Father Timothy Kavanagh, one of the earliest risers in Mitford, did not rise so early this morning. Instead, he lay in his bed in the yellow house on Wisteria Lane and listened to the aria of his wife's whiffling snore, mingled with the sound of rain churning through the gutters.

Had he exchanged wedding vows before the age of sixty-two, he might have taken the marriage bed for granted after these seven years. Instead, he seldom awakened next to the warm sentience of his wife without being mildly astonished by her presence, and boundlessly grateful. Cynthia was his best friend and boon companion, dropped from the very heavens into his life, which, forthwith, she had changed utterly.

He would get up soon enough and go about his day, first hying with his good dog, Barnabas, into the pouring rain, and then, while the coffee brewed, reading the Morning Office, as he'd done for more than four decades as both a working and a now-retired priest.

Feeling a light chill in the room, he scooted over to his sleeping wife and put his arm around her and held her close, comforted, as ever, by the faint and familiar scent of wisteria.

Lew Boyd, who liked to rise with the sun every morning, and who always wore his watch to bed, gazed at the luminous face of his Timex and saw that it was the first day of October.

October! He had no idea at all where the time had gone. Yesterday was July, today was October. As a matter of fact, where had his life gone?

He stared at the bedroom ceiling and pondered a question that he'd never been fond of messing with, though now seemed a good time to do it and get it over with.

One day, he'd been a green kid without a care in the world. Then, before you could say Jack Robinson, he'd looked up and found he was an old codger with a new and secret wife living way off in Tennessee with her mama, and him lying here in this cold, lonesome bed just as he'd been doing all those years as a widower.

He tried to recall what, exactly, had happened between his youth and old age, but without a cup of coffee at the very least, he was drawing a blank.

Though he'd worked hard and saved his money and honored his dead wife's memory by looking at her picture on Sunday and paying to have her grave weed-eated, he didn't know whether he'd made a go of it with the Good Lord or not.

For the few times he'd cheated somebody down at his Exxon station, he'd asked forgiveness, even though he'd cheated them only a few bucks. He'd also asked forgiveness for the times he'd bitten Juanita's head off without good reason, and for a few other things he didn't want to think about ever again.

To top that off, he'd quit smoking twelve years ago, cut out the peach brandy he'd fooled with after Juanita passed, and increased what he put in the plate on the occasional Sundays he showed up at First Baptist.

But the thing was, it seemed like all of it—good and bad, up and down, sweet and sour—had blown by him like Dale Earnhardt Jr. at Talladega.

He sighed deeply, hauled himself out of bed, and slid his cold feet into the unlaced, brown and white spectators he wore around the house. If Juanita was alive, or if Earlene was here, he'd probably turn on the furnace out of common decency. But as long as he was boss of the thermostat, he'd operate on the fact that an oil furnace was money down the drain and wait 'til the first hard freeze to make himself toasty.

Sitting on the side of the bed and covering his bare legs with the blanket, he scratched his head and yawned, then reached for the cordless and punched redial.

When his wife, living with her dying

mama in a frame house on the southern edge of Knoxville, answered the phone, he said, "Good mornin', dumplin.'"

"Good mornin' yourself, baby. How're you feelin' this mornin'?"

"Great!" he said. "Just *great!*"

He thought for a split second he was telling a bald-faced lie, then realized he was telling the lawful truth. It was the sound of Earlene's cheerful voice that had changed him from an old man waking up in a cold bed to a young buck who just remembered he was driving to Tennessee in his new Dodge truck, tonight.

At six-thirty, Hope Winchester dashed along Main Street under a red umbrella. Rain gurgled from the downspouts of the buildings she fled past and flowed along the curb in a bold and lively stream.

To the driver of a station wagon heading down the mountain, the figure hurrying past the Main Street Grill was but a splash of red on the canvas of a sullen, gray morning. Nonetheless, it was a splash that momentarily cheered the driver.

Hope dodged a billow of water from the wheels of the station wagon and clutched even tighter the pocketbook containing three envelopes whose contents could change her life forever. She would line them up on her desk in the back room of the bookstore and prayerfully examine each of these wonders again and again. Then she would put them in her purse at the end of the day and take them home and line them up on her kitchen table so she might do the same thing once more.

UPS had come hours late yesterday with the books to be used in this month's promotion, which meant she'd lost precious time finishing the front window and must get at it this morning before the bookstore opened at ten. It was, after all, October first—time for a whole new window display, and the annual Big O sale.

All titles beginning with the letter *O* would be twenty percent off, which would get Wesley's students and faculty hopping! Indeed, September's Big S sale had increased their bottom line by twelve percent over last year, and all because she, the usually reticent Hope Winchester, had urged the owner to give a percentage off that really "counted for something." It was a Books-A-Million, B&N, Sam's Club kind of world, Hope insisted, and a five-percent dribble here and there wouldn't work anymore, not even in Mitford, which wasn't as sleepy and innocuous as some people liked to think.

She dashed under the awning, set her streaming umbrella down, and jiggled the key in the door of Willard Porter's old pharmacy, now known as Happy Endings Books.

The lock had the cunning possessed only by a lock manufactured in 1927.

Helen, the owner, had refused to re-place it, insisting that a burglar couldn't possibly outwit its boundless vagaries.

Jiggling diligently, Hope realized that her feet were cold and soaking wet. She supposed that's what she deserved by wearing sandals past Labor Day, some-thing her mother had often scolded her for doing.

Once inside, and against the heartfelt wishes of Helen, who lived in Florida and preferred to delay heating the shop until the first snow, Hope squished to the thermostat and looked at the tem-perature: fifty degrees. Who would read a book, much less buy one, at fifty degrees?

As Margaret Ann, the bookstore cat, wound around her ankles, Hope turned the dial to "on."

The worn hardwood floor trembled slightly, and she heard at once the great boiler in the basement give its thunder-ous annual greeting to autumn in Mitford.

Uncle Billy Watson lay with his eyes squeezed shut and listened to the rain pounding the roof of the Mitford town museum, the rear portion of which he and Rose called home.

He was glad it was raining, for two reasons.

One, he figured it would make the ground nice and soft to plant th' three daffodil bulbs Dora Pugh had trotted to 'is door. Th' bulbs, if they was like her seeds, wouldn't be fit to plant, but he'd give 'er one more chance to do th' honorable thing an' stand by what she sold.

When he was feelin' stronger an' the doc would let him poke around outside, he knowed right where he'd plant to make the finest show—at the bottom of th' back steps, over to th' left where the mailman wouldn't tear up jack when he made 'is deliveries.

Feeling the gooseflesh rise along his

arms and legs, he pulled the covers to his chin.

Th' other good thing about the rain, if hit lasted, was when Betty Craig come to nurse 'im t'day, she'd be cookin' all manner of rations to make a man's jaws water. If they was anything better'n hearin' rain on th' roof an' smellin' good cookin' at the same time, he didn't know what hit'd be.

He lay perfectly still, listening now to the beating of his heart.

His heart wasn't floppin' around this-away and thataway n' more, he reckoned the pills was workin'.

In a little bit, he rolled over and covered his ears to shut out the sound of his wife's snoring in the next bed.

He might've lost a good deal of eyesight an' some control of 'is bladder, don't you know, but by jing, 'is hearin' could still pick up a cricket in th' grass, thank th' Lord an' hallelujah.

"Check this out," said J. C. Hogan, editor of the *Mitford Muse* and longtime regular of the Main Street Grill. He thrust a copy of the *Muse,* hot from his pressroom above their heads, under Father Tim's nose.

"Photo staff?" asked Father Tim.

EXPECT A SPECTACLE

As Mitford's mayor, Andrew Gregory, doesn't return until after press time from a buying trip to England, the Muse called on former mayor Esther Cunningham to make the Muse's official annual prediction about our fall leaf display.

"Color out the ka-zoo!" stated Ms. Cunningham.

Meterologists across western North Carolina agree. They say that color this fall will be "the best in years," due to a hot, dry mountain summer followed by heavy rains, which began September 7 and have continued

with some frequency.
So load your cameras and wait for Mitford's famed sugar maples, planted from First Baptist all the way to Little Mitford Creek, to strut their stuff. Color should be at its height October 10–15.
Use ASA 100 film and don't shoot into the sun. Best morning photo op: from the steps of First Baptist, pointing south. Best afternoon op: from the sidewalk in front of the church, pointing east. This advice courtesy the Muse photo staff.

"You're lookin' at it," said J.C.

"I thought you had spellcheck."

"I do have spellcheck."

"It's not working."

"Where? What?" J.C. grabbed the newspaper.

"*Meteorologist* is misspelled." The former rector of the local Episcopal church had kept his mouth shut for years about the *Muse* editor's rotten spelling, but since the newspaper had invested in spellcheck, he figured he could criticize without getting personal.

J.C. muttered a word not often used in the rear booth.

"You ought to have a photo contest," said Father Tim, blowing on a mug of steaming coffee. "Autumn color, grand prize, second prize . . . like that."

"Unless th' rain lets up, there'll be nothing worth enterin' in a contest. Besides, I'd have to shell out a couple hundred bucks to make that deal work."

"Where's Mule?" asked Father Tim. The erstwhile town realtor had been meeting them in the rear booth for two decades, seldom missing their eight a.m. breakfast tryst.

"Down with th' Mitford Crud. Prob'ly comes from that hot, dry spell changin' into a cold, wet spell."

Velma Mosely skidded up in a pair of

silver Nikes. "Looks like th' Turkey Club's missin' a gobbler this mornin'. What're y'all havin'?"

This was Percy and Velma Mosely's final year as proprietors of the Grill. After forty years, they were hanging it up at the end of December, and not re-newing the lease.

In the spring, they would take a bus to Washington and see the cherry blos-soms. Then they planned to settle into retirement in Mitford, where Percy would put in a vegetable garden for the first time in years and Velma would adopt a shorthaired cat from the shelter.

Father Tim nodded to J.C. "You or-der first."

"Three eggs scrambled, with grits, bacon, and a couple of biscuits! And give me plenty of butter with that!"

The *Muse* editor looked at Velma, ex-pectant.

"Your wife said don't let you have grits and bacon, much less biscuits an' plenty of butter." J.C.'s wife, Adele, was

Mitford's first and, so far, only police-woman.

"My *wife?*"

"That's right. Adele dropped in on her way to the station this mornin'. She said Doc Harper told you all that stuff is totally off-limits, startin' today."

"Since when is it th' business of this place to meddle in what people order?"

"Take it or leave it," said Velma. She was sick and tired of J. C. Hogan boss-ing her around and biting her head off for the last hundred years.

J.C.'s mouth dropped open.

"I'll order while he's rethinking," said Father Tim. "Bring me the usual."

Velma glared at the editor. "If you'd order like th' Father here, you'd live longer." She felt ten feet tall telling this grouchy so-and-so what was what, she should have done it years ago.

"I wouldn't eat a poached egg if somebody paid me cash money. Give me three eggs, scrambled, with grits, bacon . . ." J.C. repeated his order loud and clear, as if Velma had suddenly gone deaf. "*. . . an' two dadgum biscuits.*"

Father Tim thought his boothmate's face was a readout of his blood pressure rating—roughly 300 over 190.

"If you want to drop dead on th' street, that's your business," said Velma, "but I won't be party to it. Get you some yogurt and fresh fruit with a side of dry toast."

"This is dadblame *illegal!* You can't tell me what to order."

"Suit yourself. I promised Adele, and I'm stickin' to it."

J.C. looked at Father Tim to confirm whether he was hearing right. Father Tim looked at Velma. Maybe this was a joke. . . .

But Velma was a brick wall, an Army tank. End of discussion.

J.C. drew himself up and played his trump card. "Do I need to remind you that *this* is a *democracy?*"

Velma glared at the editor over her half-glasses; heads turned in their direction. "Where's Percy this mornin'?" demanded J.C. He would call in the troops and nip this nonsense in the bud once and for all.

"Down with th' Mitford Crud!" snapped Velma.

The young man at the grill turned his back on the whole caboodle, lest he be drawn into the altercation.

There was a long moment of silence, the sort that Father Tim never enjoyed.

"Then I'll just take my business down th' street!"

J.C. grabbed his briefcase and blew out of the rear booth like a cannon shot. Father Tim's coffee sloshed in its mug.

Roaring past the counter, the *Muse* editor peppered the air with language not fit to print and, arriving at the front door, yanked it open, turned around, and shouted, "*Which,* you may be happy to know, is where I intend to *keep* it!"

The cold rain blew in, the door slammed, the bell jangled.

"Good riddance!" said Velma, meaning it.

At the counter, Coot Hendrick dumped sugar into his coffee and stirred. "I didn't know there was anyplace down th' street to take 'is business *to.*"

"I suppose he meant the tea shop," said Luke Taylor, who hadn't looked up from his newspaper.

Guffaws. Hoots. General hilarity among the regulars. In Mitford, the Chelsea Tea Shop was definitely the province, indeed the stronghold, of the fair sex. Hardly a male had ever set foot in the place, except for a few unsuspecting tourists.

Father Tim cleared his throat. "I do think it's illegal," he said to Velma, "to refuse to . . . you know . . ."

Velma adjusted her glasses and glared at him from on high. "Since when is it illegal to save somebody's life?"

Clearly, Velma Mosely was ready for retirement.

It was one of those rare days when he sensed that all the world lay before him, that it was indeed his oyster.

Upon leaving the Grill, he stood beneath the green awning, scarcely knowing which way to turn. Though the chilling rain continued to fall and the uproar between Velma and J.C. had definitely been unpleasant, he felt light; his feet barely touched the ground. How could someone his age feel so expectant and complete? How indeed? It was the grace of God.

"Lord, make me a blessing to someone today!"

He uttered aloud his grandmother's prayer, raised his umbrella, and, beneath the sound of rain thudding onto black nylon, turned left and headed to Lord's Chapel to borrow a volume of Jonathan Edwards from the church library.

"Father!"

Andrew Gregory's head poked from the door of the Oxford Antique Shop. "Stop in for a hot cocoa."

Hot cocoa!

He hadn't tasted the delights of hot cocoa since the Boer War. In truth, the phrase was seldom heard on anyone's lips—the going thing today was an oversweet and synthetic chocolate powder having nothing to do with the real thing.

"Bless my soul!" said Father Tim. He always felt a tad more eighteenth century when he visited the Oxford. He shunted his umbrella into an iron stand that stood ready at the door and strode into one of his favorite places in all of Mitford.

"Excuse the disarray," said Andrew, who, though possibly suffering some jet lag, never looked in disarray himself. In truth, Andrew's signature cashmere jacket appeared freshly pressed if not altogether brand-new.

"The shipment from my previous trip arrived yesterday, on the heels of my own arrival. It all looks like a jumble sale at the moment, but we'll put it right, won't we, Fred?"

Fred Addison looked up from his examination of a walnut chest and grinned. "Yessir, we always do. Good mornin', Father. Wet enough for you?"

"I don't mind the rain, but my roses do. This year, we exchanged Japanese beetles for powdery mildew. How was your garden this year?" Fred Addison's annual vegetable garden was legendary for its large size and admirable tomatoes; Father Tim had feasted from that fertile patch on several occasions.

"Had to plow it under," said Fred, looking mournful.

"Let's look for a better go of things next year."

"Yessir, that's th' ticket."

Andrew led the way to the back room, where the Oxford hot plate and coffeepot resided with such amenities as the occasional parcel of fresh scones fetched from London.

"Careful where you step," said Andrew. "I'm just unpacking a crèche I found in Stow-on-the-Wold; a bit on the derelict side. Some really odious painting of the figures and some knocking about of the plaster here and there . . ."

Father Tim peered at a motley assortment of sheep spilling from a box, an angel with a mere stub for a wing, an orange camel, and, lying in a manger of bubble wrap, a lorn Babe . . .

"Twenty-odd pieces, all in plaster, and possibly French. Someone assembled the scene from at least two, maybe three different crèches."

"Aha."

Andrew poured hot milk from a pot into a mug. "Not the sort of thing I'd usually ship across the pond, yet it spoke to me somehow."

"Yes, well . . . it has a certain charm."

"I thought someone might be willing

to have a go at bringing it 'round." Andrew handed him the mug. "There you are! Made with scalded milk and guaranteed to carry you forth with good cheer and optimism."

Coffee and cocoa, all within the span of a couple of hours. Father Tim reckoned that his caffeinated adrenaline would be pumping 'til Christmas; he felt as reckless as a sailor on leave.

Mitford's capable mayor, restaurateur, and antiques dealer beamed one of his much-lauded smiles. "Come, Father, I'll show you a few of the new arrivals—and perhaps you'll catch me up on the latest scandals in Mitford?"

"That shouldn't take long," said Father Tim.

He felt the warmth of the mug in his hands and saw the rain slanting in sheets against the display windows. Everywhere in this large room that smelled of lemon oil and beeswax was something to be admired—the patina of old walnut and mahogany, a tapestry side chair bathed in the glow of lamplight, and, over there, a stack of leather-bound books just uncrated.

He had a moment of deepest gratitude, and the odd and beguiling sense that he was on the brink of something. . . .

But what?

Something . . . *different.* Yes, that was it.

Two

*T*he day after his visit to Oxford Antiques, he realized that the angel had seized his imagination.

He was surprised by a vivid recollection of her face, which he'd found beautiful, and the piety of her folded hands and downcast eyes.

As for the missing wing, wasn't that a pretty accurate representation of most of the human horde, himself certainly included?

The image of the Babe had also come to mind. The craziness and commerce of Christmas, so utterly removed from the verity of its meaning, had served to make the bubble-wrapped figure a profoundly fitting metaphor.

He hadn't given much consideration to crèche scenes in recent years; he and

Cynthia had been making do with hers, which she'd miraculously rescued from a hither-and-yon childhood. It was an odd and poignant thing, which she'd created from scraps of yarn, felt, and straw, and included clothespin shepherds for whom, at the age of fourteen, she had sewn silk robes.

Prior to arriving in Mitford, he had used his family's Irish-made crèche, observing Anglican traditions taught him by his now-long-deceased father.

Though Matthew Kavanagh had been decidedly hostile to the church and its associations, he'd celebrated Christmas, and Christmas only, with certain feeling. And, eager to promote any stirring of his heart toward God, his wife, Madelaine, had carried forth the observance of Advent and Christmas with particular zeal.

As an only child, he, Timothy, had the privilege and pleasure of setting up the Nativity scene on the first day of Advent. He always began, as his father directed, by placing Mary and Joseph and the empty manger on top of a low bookcase in their parlor. Then he grouped the two donkeys, a doleful horse, a cow, a calf, and two sheep to one side, where they stood in a concert of expectation.

His mother and father sat in the parlor with him as he assembled the hand-carved, hand-painted figures into a scene that he tried to make fresh and different each year. During one year, he might place the horse so that it looked down on the manger. Another year, he might give the cow and calf this privilege of station.

He felt happy in bringing the small setting to life, and happier still that his usually dour and remote father seemed interested in his son's effort.

"The horse will do well there," Matthew Kavanagh might say. Or, "The manger wants less straw."

"Father likes the crèche," he said to his mother.

"Yes," she said, "he has always loved it. Your great-grandmother brought it over from Ireland, and she taught your father to set it up exactly as he's teaching you."

He remembered being thrilled by this newfound connection with his father's boyhood, and even with a great-grandmother he'd never seen. He turned his face from his mother so she couldn't look upon the pride that laid his feelings bare.

During the heady days of Advent, with its special wreath and candles, and the baking done by his mother and Peggy, the house was filled with wonderful smells. These aromas, including an ever-present fragrance of chickory coffee perking on the stove, were dense and rich; he could sometimes smell them all the way to the rabbit pen, where his best friend, Tommy Noles, came to help "feed up."

"Them little pellets go in, an' th'

same little pellets come out, 'cept in a different color," said Tommy.

"Yep."

"What're you gettin'?"

"I hope a bike. What're you gettin'?"

Tommy shrugged, looking mournful. "Prob'ly nothin'."

"Everybody gets somethin' at Christmas," he said.

"Not if they're poor, they don't."

"You're not poor."

"Becky says we are."

"But you've got a house and a barn and lots of things, even horses, and we only have rabbits." He had always wanted horses.

"We got a cow, too, an' a calf," Tommy reminded him.

"Besides, she's just your little sister. She's dumb to say that. Y'all even have a truck, and we don't have a truck, only a Buick." He had always wanted a truck.

Tommy had seemed encouraged.

Four shepherds, in the meantime, waited in the dining room on the walnut sideboard, to journey to the manger on Christmas morning. In his mother's sewing room, he knew that presents waited, too. His mother spent many hours in that room, always with the door closed, wrapping presents with yards and yards of her signature white satin ribbon and protecting with uncommon zeal the wonderful secrets that he tried diligently to puzzle out.

During the long days before Christmas, he could scarcely wait to put the Babe in the manger, and often made the trek to the silver drawer of the sideboard to peer at the infant resting safely in the bowl of a gravy ladle.

At a time when his friends had stopped believing in Santa Claus, he was still believing in the powerful reality of the small tableau—in much the same way, he supposed, that a boy believes his action heroes to be living, and the battles on the parlor floor to be real.

Years later, he had stored the Irish crèche in the basement of the riverside rectory in Hastings, where he was rector for ten years prior to Mitford. He remembered driving home from a diocesan conference in a frightening storm, then opening his basement door and seeing the water risen above the bottom step.

Floating on the small, enclosed river in the lower portion of his house were the Nativity figures—camels without riders, shepherds without crooks, the stable with its pointed roof and fixed star, a miniature bale of sodden straw, and, here and there, a sheep or donkey along with other detritus loosed from cardboard containers and set free upon the floodwaters of southern Alabama.

He had rescued them and put them into a box and, in the upheaval following the flood, had forgotten them. When he opened the box months later, the figures were rank with a fetid damp that caused them to stick together in a mildewed and forbidding clump.

He'd felt a deep sense of loss, as well as relief, when, months later, he discovered that the movers had failed to load the box on the truck to Mitford.

Dear Hope,

Due to the serious nature of the following proposal, I'm not e-mailing or calling you. Instead, I'm allowing you ample time to consider my idea, and thereby give it the careful and positive thinking you've displayed in making Happy Endings a more profitable enterprise.

Mitford has great charm, but, as you're aware, it has distinct limitations, as well. Of the entire population, scarcely a tenth enjoys a thumping good read or has any inclination to open the covers of a book. We've had to go further and further afield to pay the rent and stock our shelves, and no coffee bar or gallery of so-called amusing greeting cards

could ever turn this distressing circumstance
around.

Your clever marketing of HE to surround-
ing communities, your committed endeavors
with the literacy council, and your develop-
ment of a rare-books business on the Internet, have certainly paid off. <u>But only to the
extent that the rent, the utilities, and your
salary are met each month, with barely
enough left to restock the shelves.</u>

In other words, though you work very
hard and have made a far better go of it
than I did while living in Mitford, the
profit margin remains slim and tenuous. I
don't enjoy telling you this, but it's best to
make a clean breast of things.

The HE lease is up at the end of December, and I've decided I simply don't wish to
carry on in Mitford. Instead, I'm inviting
you to join me at the store in Florida and
help grow the business here.

Really, my dear, I see no reason at all for
you to remain in Mitford. I assure you that
your dull and solitary life there will be replaced by a very exciting life here. And——

Peter and I have a charming guesthouse where you can live in great comfort until you get your wings!

I won't ring you for a week, as P and I shall be in the Keys, and thus you shall have every opportunity to think this through and give me the answer I hope— and indeed <u>expect</u>—to hear!

Yours fondly,
Helen

P.S. We will, of course, pay all moving expenses, which should be minimal, given your minuscule accommodations over the Tea Shop.

P.P.S. I'll contact Edith Mallory's attorneys tomorrow, with a sixty-day notice. As you're aware, the dreadful fire at Clear Day handicapped her severely, and though she's proved to be a grasping and unlovely landlord, I admit to feeling a certain pity for the poor creature.

Don't let the word out until Christmas is behind us—they'd all be wanting something for nothing, and I have no inten-

tion of putting on a going-out-of-business sale; remaining inventory will be moved here.

The first time Hope read this letter, her heart had raced with excitement. Now she felt it racing for quite another reason.

It was from fear of what lay ahead.

He had every reason in the world not to do it.

First, he'd never attempted anything like this before. Not even remotely like this.

Second, it was the sort of project Cynthia might take on and accomplish with great success, but as for himself, he had no such talent or skill—indeed, except for a fair amount of aptitude for gardening and cooking, he was all thumbs.

Third, there would hardly be enough hours left in the year to get the job done, though when he made an inquiry by phone, Andrew offered to help him every step of the way, vowing to call upon his professional resources for advice.

Fourth, the thing was too large, too out of proportion for the corner of the study: some figures were easily fifteen or sixteen inches tall.

Last, but definitely not least, he had enough to do. He was struggling with yet another piece of business for which he probably had no talent or skill—he was writing a book of essays. Truth be told, he'd hardly enjoyed a moment of writing the blasted things; he'd like to chuck the whole lot in the trash and be done with it. But, no, he'd invested untold hours. . . .

He put on his jacket and opened the door of the yellow house, inhaling the crisp morning air.

And another thing . . . there were the pulpits he'd agreed to supply before the year was out—five, total, including the Christmas Eve service at Lord's Chapel, due to Father Talbot's trip to Australia.

And what about the preparations he needed to make for his own trip? He and Cynthia would be going out to Meadowgate in mid-January, to farm-sit for Hal and Marge Owen for a year. As the farm was only fifteen minutes away, they could dash back and forth to Mitford with ease. Nonetheless . . .

Andrew Gregory was polishing a Jacobean chest when Father Tim arrived at the Oxford.

He went directly to Andrew and, without formal greeting or further deliberation, said, "I'll take it."

He thought his voice quavered a bit when he said this, as well it might.

He decided, as he walked homeward, that he wouldn't tell a soul what he'd done. Andrew had given him such a wonderful price on the crèche, he figured he could hardly afford not to buy it. Better still, the check he'd recently received from the sale of his geriatric Buick had covered the purchase, with a good deal to spare.

He was relieved. Vastly! Without this unexpected income, he would have had to spill the beans to Cynthia, as they'd lately agreed not to spend more than five hundred dollars without consulting the other.

However—hadn't his wife bought him a Mustang convertible that cost well above five hundred bucks, without saying a single word to him? And his Montblanc pen, which he'd learned cost more than some people's monthly mortgages, had also been a complete astonishment. Clearly, his wife believed that if a thing was to be a surprise, there was no cause to go prattling about it to the surprisee. Therefore, he had no intention of feeling guilty over what he fervently hoped and prayed would bring special joy to She Who Loves Surprises.

Last, but not at all least, Andrew had offered him the south end of the Oxford's back room in which to labor—"hard by the tap," as he would need water for his plasterwork.

Plasterwork!

That most daunting of proverbs came to mind: *You can't teach an old dog new tricks.*

The Enemy was after him already—he could almost smell the sulfur—but he was refusing the bait. Besides, if that adage was true, Grandma Moses would have been out of work, big time.

A shimmering October light dappled the sidewalk as he passed beneath a tree. . . .

And while he was at it, what about Michelangelo's pronouncement at the tender age of eighty-seven?

Ancora imparo! I am still learning.

He said it aloud, *"Ancora imparo!"* and walked up faster, humming a little.

Dear Hope,

*You are faithfully in my prayers, as prom-
ised when I left Mitford. It is a great loss, I
know, and I thank God that you now have
His strength in your life. You will find in
the days and months ahead that He will
help you bear the sadness and lead you
through the grieving with tenderness and
grace. From the horrendous experience of
losing three of my grandparents at once, I
can truthfully say there will even be times
when He blesses you with a certain joy.*

*My grandmother, Leila, is like a lamp
with an eternal wick, and a great
encouragement to everyone in her nursing
home. Naturally, I went into my work mode
and had them dancing on Wednesday, making pizzas on Thursday, and producing a
talent show on Friday. I wish you could
have seen the guy, ninety years old, who
played a harmonica—he was <u>great</u>. They're
all exhausted from my visit, and so are
Luke and Lizzie, who have done double
time. I'm really glad I came, and will tell*

you all about it when we get back. Thanks
for praying for our trip, I really appreciate it.

I think about you a lot. Remember to
save some time for me to take you to dinner
when I come home to Mitford next week.

In His mercy,
Scott

In the back room of Happy Endings, Hope finished reading the second letter on her desk and held it for a moment close to her heart. She had never received a love letter before.

She was, of course, the only one who would think it a love letter, as there was no mention of love in it, at all. Yet she could feel love beating in each word, in every stroke of the pen, just as it beat in the heart and soul of the chaplain of Hope House and expressed itself in everything he did.

Scott Murphy was practically famous for the wonderful projects he encouraged the nursing home residents to do up at Hope House, like working an annual vegetable garden that donated produce to a food pantry for area churches. Then there were his Jack Russell terriers, Luke and Lizzie, whose job it was to make the elderly residents laugh.

Hope had no idea why God had caused this wonderful thing to happen to her—someone who had hardly ever felt pretty, though she'd often been told that she was; someone who, at the age of thirty-seven, had never been in love, though she had always wanted to be and twice, mistakenly, thought she was.

But maybe she was getting ahead of herself; after all, she had been out with Scott Murphy only three times.

"So what do you think?" he asked Mule Skinner over breakfast at the Grill.

"Beats me," said Mule. "I'm sure not

drivin' to Wesley for some overpriced lunch deal."

"I saw him on the street yesterday. He suggested we meet him down at the tea shop."

"J.C.'s hangin' out at th' *tea shop?*" Mule's eyebrows shot skyward.

"Actually, he hasn't had the guts to go there yet—he's been packing a sandwich—but he said he'd do it if we'd go with him."

"Percy won't like us goin' down th' street."

"Right. True." The owner of the Grill thought he also owned his regulars. One underhanded meal at another eatery was grimly tolerated, but two was treason, with scant forgiveness forthcoming.

"I double dare you," said Mule.

Father Tim dipped his toast into a poached egg and considered this. Buying the crèche had made him feel slightly reckless. . . .

"I will if you will," he said, grinning.

At the Oxford, he and Fred unpacked the last of the figures and lined them up along the far wall of the back room. "What do you think?" he asked Fred.

Looking soberly at the lineup, Fred pondered his reply for some time. "Wellsir, you've got your work cut out for you."

Two angels, one with a missing wing. A camel with a single ear. Two sheep minus tails, and the whole flock painted a deadly chalk white. A donkey painted black, eyes and all, and looking like a lump of coal. One shepherd in decent repair, with the exception of damage to a hand that had removed three fingers; the other shepherd painted a wretched iron gray—skin, robes, shoes, and all.

The three kings had hardly fared better. In what biblical scholars generally conceded was a two-year journey to the Child, one fellow had lost a nose, another was missing part of his crown, and all were painted something akin to a mottled, industrial teal. What could Andrew have been thinking?

The Virgin Mary's bright red robe with orange undergarments was a definite redo, and indeed, the angels' gear was hardly an improvement—both wore robes in a ghastly saffron color, only a shade removed from the hue of their skin. One needn't be Leonardo da Vinci to see that the whole parcel needed redemption, save for the Babe, whose figure in the attached manger was amazingly unharmed, and not badly painted.

"Carved wood," said Andrew, peering with a loupe at a section of the small figure. "Not plaster, as I'd thought. Original paint surface, with gilt overlay. Given the wear on the gilt, perhaps mid- to late nineteenth century."

"So what do you think?" asked Father Tim, craving assurance.

"I think that as soon as I hear back

from my restoration contact in England, we should get started . . . begin at the beginning!"

"Aha," he said, feeling a dash weak in the knees.

He and Mule legged it south toward the tea shop, adrenaline pumping. Cynthia Kavanagh knew what he was up to today, and had already gotten her laugh out of it. Next, the whole town would be hee-hawing—with the exception, of course, of Percy Mosely.

In the meantime, they were Lewis and Clark, heaving off to explore a vast and unknown territory.

"You be Lewis," said Father Tim. "I'll be Clark."

"Huh?"

"And look at the timing! Cynthia says the tea shop is now serving real food, not just little sandwiches with no crusts. There's a soup of the day and dessert made in their own kitchen."

Mule looked skeptical. "Tryin' to win over th' male market, is what I heard."

"And see?" said Father Tim. "It's working!"

Dear Hope,

I was so happy when you were born. We brought you home from the hospital in a little white outfit I had knitted.

We all suffered during the years after your father died and you girls had to do without many things you wanted but you didn't complain.

Remember when you won that baking contest and bought me a wedding band because I lost mine in the laundry so long ago? I don't think I ever loved you enough, and I am sorry. I hope you will forgive me. Because you said you know God now, I hope you will be able to.

I am leaving each of you girls $5,000 in addition to the house. Your daddy's mother

*left me a little something when she died and
I never touched it even when we needed it for
your college education. I always had a feeling
you would need it more for something else.*

*I'm afraid I won't make it but please
don't cry over me. You girls be good to each
other.*

Love, Mother
Dictated to Amanda Rush, R.N.

"I left my glasses back at th' office,"
said J.C. "Somebody read me what's on
this pink menu deal."

"Let's see." Mule adjusted his glasses.
"Chicken salad with grapes and nuts.
That comes with toast points."

"Toast points? I'm not eatin' toast
points, much less anything with grapes
and nuts."

"Here's a crepe," said Father Tim,
pronouncing it in the French way. "It's
their house specialty."

"What's a krep?" asked Mule.

"A thin pancake rolled around a fill-ing."

"A filling of what?" J.C. wiped his forehead with a paper napkin.

"Shredded chicken, in this case."

"A pancake rolled around shredded chicken? Why shred chicken? If God wanted chicken to be *shredded . . .*"

"I could gnaw a table leg," said Mule. "Let's get on with it."

"I can't eat this stuff. It's against my religion."

"Whoa! Here you go," said Father Tim. "They've got flounder!"

"Flounder!" J.C. brightened.

"Fresh fillet of flounder rolled around a filling of Maine cranberries and baked. This is quite a menu."

"I don't trust this place. Everything's rolled around somethin' else. No way."

"Look," said Father Tim. "Aspic! With celery and onions. Hit that with a little mayo, it'd be mighty tasty."

J.C. rolled his eyes.

"I was always fond of aspic," said Father Tim.

"You would be," snapped J.C. "Let's cut to the chase. Is there a burger on there anywhere?"

"Nope. No burger. . . . Wait a minute . . . *organic turkey burger!* There you go, buddyroe." Mule looked eminently pleased.

"I'm out of here," said J.C., grabbing his briefcase.

"Wait a dadblame minute!" said Mule. "You're th' one said meet you here. It was your big idea."

"I can't eat this stuff."

"Sure you can. Just order somethin' an' we'll have th' kitchen pour a bowl of grease over it."

"This kitchen never saw a bowl of grease, but all right—just this once. I'm definitely not doin' this again."

"Fine!" said Mule. "Great! Tomorrow we'll go back to th' Grill, and everybody'll be happy. I personally don't take kindly to change. This is up-settin' my stomach."

"I'm not goin' back and let that witch on a broom order me around."

"Hey, y'all."

They turned to see a young woman in an apron, holding an order pad. Father Tim thought her smile dazzling.

"Hey, yourself," said Father Tim.

"I'm Lucy, and I'll be your server to-day."

"All *right!*" said Mule.

"What will you have, sir?" she asked J.C.

"I guess th' flounder," grunted the editor. "But only if you'll scrape out th' cranberries."

"Yessir, be glad to. That comes with a nice salad and a roll. And since we're taking out the cranberries, would you like a few buttered potatoes with that?"

Father Tim thought J.C. might burst into tears.

"I *would!*" exclaimed the *Muse* editor. "And could I have a little butter with th' *roll?*"

"Oh, yessir, it comes with butter."

"Hallelujah!" exclaimed Mule. "An' I'll have th' same, but no butter with th' roll."

"Ditto," said Father Tim. "With a side of aspic."

"No, wait," said Mule. "Maybe I'll try it with th' cranberries. But only if they're sweet, like at Thanksgiving. . . ."

"Don't go there," said J.C. "Bring 'im th' same thing I ordered."

Father Tim didn't mention to his lunch partners that Hessie Mayhew and Esther Bolick were sitting on the other side of the room, staring at them with mouths agape.

"Seems to me," said Mule as they hot-footed north on Main Street, "that if they're goin' for th' male market, they'd change those pink curtains."

He supposed he should begin with a sheep, maybe the one painted with the iniquitous grin. . . . "Pink isn't so bad, all things considered. We have a pink bedroom."

"There's no way I'm believin' that."

"Cynthia calls it Faded Terra-Cotta.". . . *He could earn his wings with the small stuff. . . .*

"Pink is pink," said Mule. "Th' least they could do is take th' ruffles off."

"That's a thought." *What kind of paint would they be using? And brushes? And where would they get such items? He had a yard-long list of questions. . . .*

"An' maybe change th' color of th' menu to, say, the color of my sweater."

"Garage-sale brown? I don't think so."

. . . Or maybe he should begin with the shepherds, so they could be put in place the first day of Advent. . . .

"I thought th' food was pretty good," said Mule.

"Me, too.". . . *He'd have to hustle.* . . .

"But overpriced. Way overpriced. That's why th' male demographic has steered clear of th' place. We've got more sense than to shell out six ninety-five for a piece of flounder."

"We just did." *He saw the look of amazement on Cynthia's face—she was dazzled, she was thunderstruck.* . . .

"Yeah, but I won't be goin' back, will you?"

"We'll see."

"So what're you doin' th' rest of th' day?"

What could he say? That he was starting work on the crèche? He couldn't say that. Nor could he say that in the evening, he'd be working on his essays. Mule Skinner wouldn't know an essay if he met it on the street.

"A little of this and a little of that. The usual."

"Me, too," said Mule, who certainly

didn't want it known that he was
headed home for a long nap.

He looked at his watch. If he scurried,
he could trot to Happy Endings and get
back to the Oxford for an hour and a
half before picking up Cynthia at the
car dealership in Wesley.

"Any books with the Nativity scene,
or about Nativity scenes in general,
or . . . like that?"

"No, sir, not right now," said Hope,
"but our Christmas stock is starting to
come in."

Margaret Ann, who moused for her
bed and board, stood up from the sales
counter and stretched, then padded
over to him and licked his hand.
Though he wasn't immensely fond of
cats, they seemed to take to him with
alacrity.

"I'd like to see, for example, what
color the robes of angels might be."
Hadn't he received literally thousands

of Christmas cards over the years, many featuring angels? Yes. But could he remember the fine particulars of their robes? No.

"Robes of angels," Hope said aloud, taking notes. "What else, Father?"

"I'd like to see some wise men while I'm at it, and shepherds. A few camels and donkeys wouldn't hurt, either."

"You're having a Christmas tableau at your church?"

"A tableau, yes, but not necessarily at church." He could see, up front, that keeping this thing secret would have its pitfalls. He would have to be careful, always, to tell the truth, even while avoiding it.

"I think I know just what you need. It's a beautiful picture book with lots of artists' renderings of the Holy Family and the Nativity. In color! Shall I order it for you?"

Hope's eyes were bright behind the lenses of her tortoiseshell-frame glasses.

"Please! Would you? I need it ASAP."

"Consider it done!" she said, quoting one of his own lines. "I'll have them ship it two-day air."

"While we're at it, Hope, let me tell you how much Cynthia and I appreciate the great job you're doing here. You've turned Happy Endings into a bookstore we're all proud of."

Her eyes suddenly flooded with tears. "Thank you," she whispered.

"You and your sister, Louise, are faithfully in my prayers," he assured her. "I'm sorry about the loss of your mother."

"Thank you," she said again.

"Let me pray for you."

"Yes."

He reached across the counter and took her hand, and held it.

He thumbed through his engagement calendar with his right hand while holding a mug of hot tea in his left. A cold wind had come up, causing a

branch of the red maple to lash against
the guttering.

Let's see, he was celebrating at St.
Paul's on Sunday next, then at St.
Stephen's two weeks further. He could
use a tad of help from his erstwhile sec-
retary, but she was in Atlanta through
Christmas, helping monitor her daughter's high-risk pregnancy.

They were racing toward the holidays, into the time when Dooley
would be home from the University
of Georgia, and Dooley's long-lost
younger brother, Sammy, would join
them at the yellow house for Thanksgiving dinner. He sat back and closed
his eyes, and warmed both hands on
the mug.

He remembered the first time he ever
saw Dooley Barlowe—barefoot, unwashed, and looking for a place to
"take a dump." He chuckled. How
could he ever have guessed that this
thrown-away boy, then eleven years
old and now twenty, would change his

heart, his life, for all time? But Dooley wasn't the only thrown-away Barlowe—three brothers and a sister had been let go by their mother, and it had long been his personal mission to find them all, to see the sundered nest made whole.

On Thanksgiving Day, four of the five siblings would break bread together at the Kavanagh board. Only Kenny remained lost to them, and only God knew where he might be found.

Three

*U*ncle Billy Watson shuffled to the chair by the kitchen window and peered out to his yard at the north end of Main Street.

The boys from town hall had come by to cut grass, but had jumped in their truck and roared off before he could holler at them to come hear his new joke. He'd found it in a periodical that Betty Craig brought, and had studied it out in the night when his wife's snoring had kept him awake.

He squinted through the panes of the upper sash.

Th' dern jacklegs had come through th' yard a-flyin,' an' left th' grass a-layin' in rows ever'whichaway. Triflin' is what it was, th' way th' town let th' weeks go by between mowin's, then was too shif'less t' rake th' leavin's!

He wouldn't've told 'em 'is new joke, nohow.

He clutched at his heart. There it was, flipping around like a catfish on a riverbank.

"Lord, I've give up on them boys, don't You know, but You ain't. I hope You won't give up on me, amen."

He fiddled with the window sash and finally raised it about a foot, then thumped into his chair and propped his cane against the wall. He figured if he sat here long enough, somebody would walk by on the street, and he'd call them over an' fire off his joke.

Trouble was, they didn't nobody walk n'more; seem like every dadjing one of 'em had a vehicle, which they drove aroun' th' monument like they was goin' to a Democrat barbecue. These days, about th' only people a man could see a-walkin' was preachers—Preacher Kavanagh with 'is big black dog, an' Preacher Sprouse with 'is new dog that trotted sideways like a crab.

Either more people needed t' git 'em a dog—or more people needed t' go into preachin'.

Here it was October, an' th' trees was colorin' up good since th' rain. Pretty soon, Thanksgivin' would be along, then hit'd be Christmas, don't you know.

He recollected th' stockin's him and Maisie used to git. He wished that one more time he'd git a stockin' with a orange an' a hard candy an' maybe a little horse whittled out of a pine knot. Yessir, that'd be a treat.

This year, he didn't have no idea a'tall what to give Rose f'r Christmas. Ever' year 'bout this time, he already had it studied out, which give him more'n two months to hand-make 'is present.

For a good while, he'd built 'er a birdhouse, seein' as she was tenderhearted about birds. They was sixteen or seventeen birdhouses he'd nailed around the yard over th' years, but th' town had tore ever' one of 'em down when they fixed their two front rooms to be th' museum.

"Rotted!" was what the town boys had said.

A man went down th' street to Dora Pugh's an' got 'im a mite of lumber an' nails an' what all, an' toted it home and built a fine birdhouse an' painted th' roof an' all, an' put a little peg under th' hole so th' bird would have a place to set an' all, and what happens? Hit *rots!* They was no use to th' whole dadjing business.

It was queer th' way Rose was s' mean about ever'thing a man could think of, and then, come Christmas, she was google-eyed as a young 'un.

More'n once she'd come over an' hugged 'is neck.

"What's 'at f'r?" he'd ask.

"For being Bill Watson!" she'd say, grinnin' to beat th' band.

Of course, she'd also said, "Don't you make me any more birdhouses, Bill Watson, do you hear?"

Unlike hisself, Rose was educated. When she laid down the' law, he always listened and tried to mind. That's why he might as well git his mind off of birdhouses an' onto somethin' like . . . like what?

B'fore 'is arthur had got s' bad, he'd one year caned th' bottom of 'er kitchen chair, an' another year he'd made a little bread box with a knob he'd whittled in th' shape of a squirrel.

He searched around in his mind for something to do this year.

But nossir, they wasn't a single notion in 'is noggin. He shook his head to see if anything rattled; maybe his brain had rotted.

He'd figure it out, somehow; he'd come up with somethin'. Hit would make 'is ol' heart happy t' have Rose huggin' 'is neck ag'in.

In a little bit, he'd git up an' peel his-

self a Rusty Coat—it had growed on
th' gnarly ol' tree he'd planted out back
when they was married. Hit'd keep th'
doc away, is what his mama always said.
An' if they was anything he wanted f'r
Christmas more'n a stockin' an' a hug
from Rose, hit was t' keep th' doc
away.

Hope thought at first it might be the
hot jasmine tea, or even the letter from
Scott. Then she realized the true iden-
tity of the warm, almost breathless feeling. Though similar to the emotion she
had when she prayed that prayer with
George Gaynor on the phone, this was
by no means so powerful or disarming.
Still, her head felt slightly dizzy. . . .

She set the cup in the saucer and
stared out the window, unseeing. There
was a growing certainty that the flushed
feeling was, in fact, an idea . . . an idea
that was forming not just in her head

but in her heart, and perhaps, it seemed, in the very depths of her soul.

He'd thought it all through, and, yes, he wanted to begin the Advent season by setting the shepherds on his own sideboard—something he figured he could do without giving away the entire surprise.

"What about starting with the shepherds?" he asked Fred, who, though younger than himself, had suddenly become a wise elder, a veritable sage on the mount.

Fred pulled at his chin, thoughtful. "I wouldn't tackle that straight off." He pointed to the figures lined up along the rear wall. "One of your fellas is missin' part of a hand, th' other one's stubbed his toe, an' th' way they're painted, both of 'em has a mean look."

"Yes, of course. You're right." How would he ever form a hand from plaster? He supposed he would profit by using the other hand as a model—but all those fingers—and how would he change mean looks? He'd never painted anything before.

His heart sank; he felt a kind of suffocation in his chest. Why was he so infernally inclined to jump off cliffs with nothing to break his fall? "Is there anything I could do today in, say, an hour or so? I have a dental appointment in Wesley."

"I think a good washin' up would be in order. Your paint'll get a better purchase on a clean surface. Which reminds me, Mr. Gregory says your paints an' all should be in tomorrow, along with that English fella's advice on how to get th' job done."

Advice on how to get the job done! He distinctly felt some of the pressure lift off his chest. He would set aside the entire day tomorrow; enough, already, with the business of an hour here, an hour there.

They heard the bell jangle on the front door.

"Th' soap's under the sink," said Fred, hurrying from the room.

He squatted down and found the soap, a foul-smelling block with the heft of a brick and the color of peat. Where to begin? At the beginning, of course.

He walked over and hoisted the donkey from the front of the lineup and was coming back to the sink when a head poked around the door. "Father?"

He froze, caught in the act. He'd failed to tell Fred this was a covert enterprise.

"Hope!"

"I just saw Mr. Skinner, and he said you'd gone down to the Oxford, so I took a quick break to deliver your book."

She clutched it to her heart in a mailing wrapper. "I hope it's what you wanted."

"I'm sure it will be. Umm, look, Hope . . ."

"What an interesting Nativity group! My goodness, how many pieces?"

"Please, Hope, what I'm doing is a secret. That is, I don't want anyone to know. . . . I'm going to try to restore the whole caboodle. . . . It's a surprise for my wife . . . a *surprise.*"

"Oh, no, I would never say a word, I promise." Secrets were nothing new to a bookseller. . . ."Are you going to restore *all* this?"

"Yes," he said. "By the grace of God."

"Would you like me to open your book? I can see why you need it!"

"Well, yes, thank you, and I'll just go on with my work." He let out his breath; he could trust Hope.

As she tore into the book wrapping, he set the donkey in the sink and turned on the warm water and dunked the rag and scoured it over the soap and went to work on the grimy figure.

"Here we are!" she said, looking happy. "I'll hold it up for you and turn the pages."

"Good idea! Many hands make light work!" He scrubbed away, the water turning black.

"You were interested in angels' robes, as I recall. This angel is lovely, don't you think? Its robe appears to be painted with several shades of blue, and look, there's this wonderful rose-colored undergarment. . . ."

"It's sporting white wings into the bargain. I think I like white wings best." His particular crowd appeared grimly earthbound with their saffron-colored appendages.

She turned the page. "Here's an angel with gold wings. I agree, Father. Definitely white! One would be hard-pressed to fly with all that gold on one's wings."

He peered at his bookseller, smiling. "I must say you're looking angelic

yourself. Radiant would be the word."
He rinsed the donkey; dirty water gurgled down the drain.

She flushed. "Thank you, Father. I have a secret, too."

"Aha."

"But I can't tell you what it is."

"Of course you can't, because then it wouldn't be a secret."

"I need you to pray."

He finished drying the donkey with a paper towel. "Consider it done."

"God has just given me the most wonderful idea."

"He does that sort of thing."

"But it's frightening. I mean, it's frightening and then it's . . . it's so exciting that I can hardly sleep. It seems such a huge thing, and I've never done a huge thing before." She took a deep breath. "I've always done . . . small things."

"I understand."

"You do?"

"Oh, yes."

"It seems nearly impossible."

"Ah."

"Would you ask God to give me wisdom? Would you ask Him to . . . guide and direct me in this?"

"I must say, for a brand-new believer, you have a clear understanding of what to ask for. And, yes, I will pray."

"I don't know if I can do it," she said, looking anxious. "All I know is that I want to do it . . . very much."

He stood at the sink, holding the donkey. "Don't worry about anything, Hope, but in everything, by prayer and supplication, with thanksgiving, make your requests known unto God, and the peace that passes all understanding will fill your heart and mind through Christ Jesus."

"Brilliant," she said. "Thank you!"

"Not my words. St. Paul's. Philippians four, verses six and seven."

"Four, six and seven," she repeated.

"I'll remember." She looked around the room and then at him. "I like your secret."

He grinned. "I have a feeling I'm going to like yours, as well."

"I must hurry back, Father. Do come up to our sale!" She laid his book on the chair. "It's twenty percent off any title beginning with *O*."

"*The Old Man and the Sea*?" He'd never read it, shame on him. "Or does the *The* count against me?"

"No, sir, the *The* doesn't count against you. But it's sold out! The college, you know. I can order it, though."

"No, no. Let's see, then . . . *The Original Christmas Gift*?"

"Albert Lawrence Jr.?"

"The same!"

"I have one copy."

"Well done!" he said. "And remember: Worry about nothing, pray about everything." He'd gotten this message from a wayside pulpit somewhere—a sermon and a half in a half dozen words, and a splendid exegesis of the Philippians passage.

When she left, he discovered a lighter feeling in the province of his heart.

He trotted to the lineup, set down the donkey, and snatched up a shepherd.

He walked from the garage, whistling.

Rolling up his sleeves and giving that crowd a bath had helped endow him with the confidence he'd lacked. As he handled the figures, one by one, they seemed to grow familiar and less intimidating.

He quoted Horace aloud as he opened the door. "'He who has begun is half done.'"

Risotto! He smelled it at once.

It was currently his favorite comfort food, though decidedly one notch below a cake of hot, golden-crusted cornbread with plenty of butter.

He could eat risotto only occasionally and, alas, only sparingly. As diabetics had learned the hard way, rice, pasta, or potatoes turned at once to sugar when they hit the bloodstream.

Barnabas followed him along the hall to the kitchen, where Cynthia looked up in mid-stir. "Timothy!"

Seeing his blond wife at the stove never failed to inspire him—not only was she a leading children's book author and illustrator, she was a dab hand at cookery and plenty good-looking into the bargain. And to think that the urbane Andrew Gregory had pursued her while he, a country parson and rustic rube, had won her. . . .

"Marry me!" he said, standing behind her and nuzzling her hair.

She peered into the pot and, satisfied, replaced the lid. "It's lovely of you to ask, sir, but you're entirely too late. I'm happily wed to a retired priest."

"Must be dull as dishwater living with the old so-and-so."

"Never dull," she murmured, turning to kiss him on the cheek.

"What, then?"

"Peaceful! You see, he's gone much of the time, or working away in his study. Always up to something, that fellow."

"Speaking of being up to something, how's the angel-tree project shaping up?"

"It's Mitford's first ecumenical angel tree, and the first to collect nothing but food for Christmas dinner. Families will each get two bags of groceries, including a turkey. Everything will be stockpiled at the fire station and distributed from there."

"Good thinking."

"Hundreds of families in this part of the county will be guaranteed a wonderful meal, but heaven knows . . ." She rolled her eyes.

"Heaven knows what?"

"It will take a monumental effort to scrape all our churches together in one accord."

"Better you than me!"

"Besides, we should have started last

year. We'll be working like mad for weeks."

"I'm proud of you," he said, giving her his best hug. *Risotto!*

"Ugh, you smell like some dreadful soap. What have you been *doing?*"

"A little of this and a little of that. The usual."

She peered at him, raising an eyebrow. "The usual?"

She would nail him if he didn't watch out. All right, then, he would give her a clue, but only one, and not a jot nor a tittle more.

"Christmas is coming, you know."

She laughed. "Which, of course, explains everything!"

When the phone rang, he made an effort to get to it quickly—the caller could, after all, be his boy, who sometimes checked in between morning classes.

Good grief, it was eight o'clock; it

wouldn't be Dooley at all. And why in heaven's name was he lolling about in bed at eight in the morning? And where was his wife?

"Hello!" he said, feeling unsteady on his feet.

"Father, it's Andrew."

"Andrew, what is it?" The mayor sounded as if he were speaking from a deep hole.

"I know you wanted to work at the shop today, and I certainly wanted to help you. But I'm down with what is indelicately referred to as . . ."

"Not the Mitford Crud?"

"One and the same. So let's reschedule, shall we? I'll give you a ring when I'm out and about; Fred will have his hands full."

Andrew sneezed.

"Bless you," said Father Tim.

He made straight for his wing chair, and thumped into it. He had only just noticed that his head felt clogged, rather like a drainpipe that had taken on a sock. There was also a sort of gurgling going on in his stomach.

No! Absolutely not.

He would have none of it, *none* of it! He shook a feeble fist into the air.

He leaned back to catch his breath from the rude awakening, then bolted suddenly from the chair and lurched toward their bathroom.

The door was locked.

"I can't come out, Timothy, I'm feeling terrible!"

He raced downstairs and tilted into the powder room, and not a moment too soon.

"Hey, sugar!" said Lew.

"Oh, hey, baby, I'm glad it's you, I was just takin' Mama's supper up. Let me call you back, I want her to have it while it's hot—it's Miz Paul's fish sticks, her favorite, an' a little applesauce, not too sweet."

"Fine."

He didn't even say "I love you," which is what he usually said to his wife before hanging up. He just hung up, period. He was shot from a day of pumping gas and jiving around with everybody and his brother, and coming home to nothing but a broken-down TV that only got three channels. And not that he was having a big pity party or anything, but her mama was getting hot fish sticks while he was firing up a can of Bush's baked beans on a stove with only two working burners.

How long was he willing to live like this?

"Married an' livin' single!" he hollered down the dark hallway.

Nothing had changed since Juanita passed. The dining room was still full of everything from a fake Christmas tree to a Santa Claus that dropped his pants while a music box played, not to mention empty cartons stacked to the ceiling and enough tinsel to sink a trawler.

His oven ran cold and his thermostat ran hot, and his wife lived with her mama, and every night of his life since Juanita died seven years ago, he'd come home to an empty kitchen and an empty bed, and what was the dadblame use of it all, anyhow?

He sighed and looked around at a room that had frozen in time, inside a house that had frozen with it.

It hit him then, like a bolt of lightning.

He was going out tonight.

Yessir, buddyroe, he was going to Wesley, like half the Mitford population on Friday night!

First, he'd head to Wendy's for a Bacon Swiss Cheeseburger. . . .

All the way! Large fries! Large Coke! The works.

Then he was hitting the aisles at Wal-Mart for a TV and a VCR.

After Wal-Mart, he was stopping by the mall for two scoops of Rocky Road in a waffle cone. And on the way home, he'd pick up a couple of videos.

He felt his adrenaline pumping like an oil derrick.

On Monday, he was calling the cable company, trifling as they may be, and ordering the whole caboodle—whatever they had to offer, that's what he was getting, the Disney Channel, the sports network, old movies, you name it.

He went to the coat rack by the back door and put on his fleece jacket, zipped it up, and popped a toboggan on his head.

Yessir, this was the ticket. It wasn't so much that he was lacking a wife as he was lacking a *life*.

When Earlene called back after feeding her mama, she would wonder where he was. He was always home when Earlene called. He felt in his pocket for his gloves.

"I'm goin' *out*, Earlene!" he shouted

to the kitchen ceiling. "Out, out, *out!* Leave a message!"

Of the many and varied fruits of a good marriage, one of Father Tim's sworn favorites was having someone to be sick with—misery, after all, loved company.

Sitting with her cat, Violet, in her lap, his wife blew her nose and looked at him with red eyes and drooping lids. "I never heard of anything that was both viral *and* bacterial. I thought we got only one misery at a time."

"I think it's the double deal that earned the Crud its name."

"Anyway, I've finally figured out how it feels to have this pernicious blight."

"Speak," he said, lying flat and drained on the sofa.

"It feels like you've just eaten a dish of Miss Rose's week-old, unrefrigerated banana pudding and are on your way to the emergency room in the back of a van that's been lived in through a long, hard winter by seven Russian wolfhounds, all of whom, poor dears, have mange. . . ."

He moaned. Right on the money.

"*Plus,* you have this horrendous headache—*pounding,* mind you—and eyes that feel like little sockets of ground glass, something akin to the lethal shards of a Coke bottle that's been run over by a tractor trailer hurtling at great speed along I-95—"

"North or south?"

"South."

He raised his head feebly from the sofa. "I'd never have thought of it that way," he said.

He stood at their bedroom window and looked across the rooftops toward First Baptist and the regimental march of autumn color blazing east to Little Mitford Creek.

The maples were one of the town's proudest assets, and, as predicted, they were doing their thing, they were strutting their stuff, they were breaking any and all previous records.

Glorious!

He could see only the tops of these honorable trees, but it was enough to demonstrate what he was missing. Blast! The best part of autumn was passing him by, and, into the bargain, his project was moldering. . . .

"How are the trees?" Cynthia croaked from the vicinity of their bed.

"Today may be their peak," he said, wistful. How could they miss the maples? Nobody missed the maples.

"We've got to get up there, Timothy, and take pictures, I haven't missed a single year since I moved to Mitford."

"But we're still sick," he said, straggling to the bed and thumping into it. "I feel like the Coke bottle under the wheels of your tractor trailer heading north—"

"South! We'll bundle up to our ears and wear dark glasses so no one can see how frightening we look. I'll pop on my green felt hat, and you can wear your black thingamabob that transforms you into a cleric from *Barchester Towers*."

"Do we have to?" He was whining. He hated whining.

"Yes, dearest, we have to."

She plucked a tissue from her robe pocket and blew her nose. "Missing the maples would be like missing the queen riding through in a convoy. I figure we have two more days to hang around here being miserable, and by then a storm could take the leaves down and all would be lost."

"Give me ten minutes," he said. "I won't even brush my teeth."

Though they tried to keep their distance from the crowd that was buzzing around with cameras, they couldn't help overhearing what Madge Stokes and Fancy Skinner were saying.

"How long have you *had* it?" demanded Fancy, swaddled to the gills in a pink rabbit-fur jacket over stretch capris.

"Three days," said Madge, pale and cowering.

"*Three days?* You're still *contagious*, for Pete's sake, get *away* from me, oh, *please*, the Mitford *Crud* and you're out and about and *breathing on people* after only *three* days!"

"Go jump in the lake," Cynthia muttered into her coat collar.

Fancy turned from Madge Stokes, who had gone paler still, and stumped the crowd at large. "That's the way people *do* these days, they get sick as *dogs*, but nobody, and I mean *nobody*, goes to *bed* anymore and drinks plenty of *liquids*, they're all out at the *mall* or dashing around grocery stores *coughing* on the *cabbage!*"

They slunk homeward with their spent roll of Fuji.

Four

"Lookit," said Percy. "That's my shot right there."

The Main Street Grill had come up with its own photo contest—the wall to the right of the door was plastered with images of the Mitford maples, documented with varying degrees of skill.

"See th' fog? To my way of thinkin,' that gives it . . . gives it . . ."

"Mystery and intrigue!" said Father Tim.

"That's what I was goin' t' say. Look here, this is Mule and Fancy's deal. Too dark on th' left is what Velma said, like somebody was standin' in their own shadow."

"That's somebody's thumb, actually. Whose shot is that? The one up top."

"Lew Boyd."

"Lew has a camera? He never struck me as the camera type."

"Everybody's got a camera."

"Great color. And look at the way the light falls on the grass. How many entries so far?"

"Thirteen so far. I got a sign in th' window, we'll let 'er rip 'til th' end of next week."

"What's the prize?"

"Free lunch for two."

"Good deal."

"Tuesday only, an' th' winner has to claim 'is prize by Christmas Eve, or no cigar."

"Who are the judges?"

"Me an' Velma."

"You're not going to award the winner your Tuesday special, I fondly hope." Percy's fried gizzards were a prize, all right. . . .

"They can order what they want to," said Percy. "Up to a point."

"What's the point?" He was just checking.

"One entrée, one drink, and one dessert each. And by th' way, no digital doodah or color Xerox, just straight four-by-six glossy, an' print your name on th' back."

"I think I'll enter," he said.

Percy straightened his apron. "I heard you an' Mule and Whatsisface was down at the tea shop chattin' it up like a bunch of women."

"You heard right!" he said, slipping toward the rear booth.

There was a brief silence as Percy decided whether to chase that rabbit or let it go. "So what're you havin'?"

"The usual."

"I'd rather be hit upside th' head than poach eggs this mornin'."

"Come the end of December, you'll never have to poach another egg as long as you live. So cut me some slack, buddyroe."

Percy grinned, a rare and astonishing sight. "I'm getting' out of here b'fore th' end of December. We're closin' shop Christmas Eve, right behind th' last lunch customer."

"Christmas Eve?" It was all happening too fast. . . .

"Amen!" said Percy, who wasn't often given to liturgical language.

Following yet another phone talk with Helen, Hope had bared her heart to Scott Murphy over dinner the previous evening in Wesley. He had held her hand and prayed for her, right there in the restaurant.

Grateful and tremulous, she had come home to sit down with a notepad and gather her thoughts about writing to Edith Mallory, when suddenly the words began to tumble onto the page with scarcely any caution or forethought.

In the end, it had been exactly what she wanted to say.

She would transcribe the hastily composed missive to a sheet of ivory stationery and send it registered mail—something she had never before done with a document of any sort.

The only concern she had in writing the letter was whether to mention Mrs. Mallory's terrible injuries, which had rendered her unable to speak except in a fashion so garbled that not even her doctors could understand her meaning.

If no reference was made in the letter to such a tragedy, it might be construed as coldness of spirit, or worse.

She would take her cue, then, from rumor—that Mrs. Mallory was now able to communicate, though with painful slowness, to Ed Coffey, the man who had driven her around for so many years in that black Lincoln. A further rumor reported a recent removal of the bandages from Edith Mallory's head.

In this fearsome and thrilling thing she was about to do, she had every intention of looking always on the bright side.

Dear Mrs. Mallory, she penned at the top of the ivory sheet . . .

I was very happy to hear of your recent improvements, and trust that we shall have continuing good news of your recovery.

I also trust that the following proposal will meet with your deepest approval.

As you are perhaps aware, my longtime employer, Helen Huffman, has recently informed your attorney that due to pressing demands of her Florida business, she will not renew the lease on your old Porter building, long known as Happy Endings Books.

Indeed, it is my heartfelt desire to renew the lease in my own name, and to assume full responsibility as Happy Endings Books' new owner and manager.

*Mrs. Mallory, I speak to you as one busi-
nesswoman to another, and believe you will
appreciate my wish to be entirely frank.*

*The monthly lease is now $950 plus
utilities, but I will be able during the first
six months to pay only $800, plus
utilities.*

*On July first and thereafter, I expect to be
fully able to pay the monthly sum of $950
plus utilities without further hindrance.*

*In the meantime, I will, at my own ex-
pense, repaint the interior walls, which are
in sore condition, and have a new toilet and
front-door lock installed at my expense.
These improvements are worth
approximately $2,500 by today's estima-
tions, thus you would recognize a benefit of
$1,550 at the very outset of our relation-
ship.*

*I will work hard, Mrs. Mallory, to make
you proud to count Happy Endings among
your most responsible tenants. I have had a
lifelong love of learning and of books, and
cannot express to you the joy it would give
me to undertake such a rewarding*

*endeavor—an endeavor which I believe
enriches our community immeasurably.*

*Should you consider my proposal with
favor, I shall be happy to dispatch character
references at once.*

Yours sincerely,
Hope Winchester
Happy Endings Books

The effort to transcribe the letter in
ink, without making mistakes, had
been considerable. Should she have
written instead to Mrs. Mallory's attorneys? She didn't know anything about
attorneys. And should she have referred to herself as a businesswoman?
"Yes!" Helen had insisted. "Absolutely!"

She felt a heaviness between her
shoulders, as if she'd toted a barge along
Little Mitford Creek.

Slipping the folded, two-page letter
inside the envelope, she licked the seal
and considered again the ways in which

she hoped to make this impossible dream come true.

Money would be scarce, very scarce, especially as Helen would be taking fifty percent of the profits during the first year, in payment for her inventory and for revenue earned from the rare-books realm. In addition to rent and utilities, that would be a heavy outgo. As for income, she had only her mother's surprising legacy, the forty-seven hundred dollars she had saved since college, and, of course, the five hundred dollars per month she would save if . . .

She drew another sheet of paper from the box.

Dear Mrs. Havner,

Thanks to your many courtesies over the years, I have been happy in my little nest above your tea shop.

I've always been especially fond of Thursdays, for the smell of your delectable

*cinnamon rolls wafted up to my aerie and
made it all the more a true home!*

*It is with deep regret, as well as joy un-
bounded, that I write to tell you I will not
be renewing my lease this year. . . .*

She drew a shallow breath.

This letter couldn't be mailed, of
course, until she heard from Mrs. Mallory, which, she felt certain, would be
only a few days hence.

She spied the folded slip of paper that
Scott had given her, lying by the stationery box. When he walked her to
the door last night, he had proffered it
like a fortune from a cookie.

"This will help," he said, smiling. "I
promise."

She remembered the tips of his fingers brushing the palm of her hand. . . .

She unfolded the paper now and
read once again the inscription in blue
ink.

*Philippians 4:13: I can do all things
through Christ who strengthens me.*

A white cake box had been delivered while he and Cynthia were shopping at The Local.

"What is it?" he asked Puny.

He hoped to the good Lord it wasn't one of Esther's orange marmalade cakes. The angst of not being able to eat the whole thing, much less a single, solitary piece . . .

"Fruitcake!" she said, obviously disgusted. "Won't people ever learn you can't *eat* this stuff?"

"Well, yes," he said, "but Cynthia can, and you, and Dooley. A fine gift!"

"Mister Cunningham made it, it's your Christmas present. He brought it early so you can start soakin' it in bourbon or whatever. He said he was willin' to do th' bakin', but he draws th' line on soakin'."

Their housekeeper, whom he loved as his own blood, and who had stayed home until the contagion passed, was

roughly five months away from delivering a second round of twins.

"You look wonderful, Puny. How are
my new grans?"

She grinned. "Kickin'!"

"Keep doing what you're doing. I'm
going to stretch out in the study a few
minutes."

"I'm bakin' a pie with Sadie Baxter
apples an' fake sugar. I'll try not t' make
noise."

"Oh, but make noise! Rattle those
pots and pans! That's what home is
about."

A pie! He fairly skipped into the
study.

Cynthia was already prone on their
bed. Following endless days of the
Crud, the two blocks to the store and
back had been right up there with
swimming the English Channel.

His good dog heaved himself onto
the sofa and laid his head on his master's
feet.

"Barnabas," he murmured before

drowsing off to sleep, "just wait 'til you see what's coming.

"Sheep! Shepherds! A camel! Angels! You won't believe it."

"Miz Kavanagh, is it all right t' give Timothy some of this candy fruit?"

"Two cherries!" he said, extending both hands. Why did Peggy have to ask his mother everything? If it was up to Peggy, he could have almost anything he wanted.

"Please," he remembered to say.

"Very well," said his mother, "but only two."

He also wanted raisins and a brazil nut, but he would ask later. He liked a lot of things that went into the fruit-cake his mother and Peggy made every year, but he didn't like them *in* the cake, he liked them *out* of the cake.

Coffee perked on the electric range, a lid rattled on a boiling pot, he smelled cinnamon and vanilla. . . .

At the kitchen table, his mother wrote thoughtfully on a sheet of blue paper. "There'll be the Andersons, of course," she said to Peggy, "and the Adamses."

"What about th' judge?"

"The judge goes without saying. We always have the judge."

"An' Rev'ren' Simon."

"Yes, I think his influence is good for Timothy."

"Ain't you havin' th' Nelsons?"

"Oh, yes, and the Nelsons. Definitely!"

"Them Nelson boys'll be slidin' down yo' banister an' crawlin' up yo' curtains," Peggy muttered.

He didn't like the Nelson boys; when they came, it was always two against one.

"Can Tommy come?" His father had never allowed Tommy in the house, but since this would be Christmas . . .

"No, dear. I'm sorry. Perhaps another time."

His mother furrowed her brow and looked at the rain lashing the windows. Peggy stirred batter in a bowl, shaking her head.

"What shall we serve, Peggy? Certainly, we want your wonderful yeast rolls!"

"Yes, ma'am, an' Mr. Kavanagh will want his ambrosia and oyster pie."

His mother smiled, her face alight. "Always!"

"An' yo' famous *bûche de Noël!*" said Peggy. "That always get a big hand clap."

"What is boose noel?" he asked, sitting on the floor with his wooden truck.

"*Bu*oosh," said Peggy. "Bu like *bureau*. *Bu*oosh."

"Boosh."

"No, honey." Peggy bent down and stuck her face close to his. He liked Peggy's skin, it was exactly the color of gingerbread. "Look here at my lips . . . *bu* . . ."

"*Bu* . . ."

"Now . . . law, how I goin' t' say this? Say shhhh, like a baby's sleepin'."

"Shhhh."

"That's right! Now, *bu*-shhh."

"*Bu* . . . shhh."

"Run it all together, now. *Bu*shhh."

"*Bu*shhh!"

"Ain't that good, Miz Kavanagh?"

"Very good!"

Peggy stood up and began to stir again. "Listen, now, honey lamb, learn t' say th' whole thing—*bûche de Noël.*"

"*Bûche de Noël!*"

"He be talkin' French, Miz Kavanagh!"

He was thrilled with their happiness; with no trouble at all, he'd gotten raisins and a Brazil nut for talking French.

"What does it mean, Mama?"

"Log of Christmas. Christmas log. A few days before Christmas, you may help us put the icing on. It's a very special job."

"Icin' on a log?"

"A log made from cake. We had it last year, but you probably don't remember—you were little then." His mother smiled at him; he saw lights dancing in her eyes.

"Yes, ma'am, and now I'm big."

"You ain't big," crowed Peggy, "you my *baby!*"

He hated it when Peggy said that.

Don't count your chickens before they hatch.

She'd heard that all her life. But in this thing she was praying and believing could be done, she wanted to get started.

Why not spend the days of waiting, acting as if it were going to happen?

If it didn't happen, she would take the penalty of great disappointment as her just and rightful lot. Of course, if it didn't happen, what would she do? She didn't want to leave Mitford, not at all.

If Edith Mallory refused to give her

the lease, Helen's moving truck would come and everything would be crated up and taken to Florida, leaving the store empty for an as-yet-unknown occupant. She had a fleeting image of herself, standing in the middle of the large and vacant room. . . .

But, no! She mustn't think that way. How, then, might she begin acting as if it were going to happen?

"Dear God . . . ," she whispered.

No matter what the future held, the big room upstairs, long used for storage, would have to be cleaned out. She took a deep breath and allowed herself to examine again the wondrous possibilities.

In that light-filled room, there would be space for all three of her bookcases.

She would be able to use her mother's lace curtains at the windows facing Main Street—without having measured, she knew they would fit.

The faded Aubusson rug, which had

for years been her grandest possession, would look beautiful on the old pine floor.

Though customers had come in, she raced up the stairs to look again at the room with its three handsome, albeit unwashed, windows.

Halfway along the stairs, she paused.

What would she do for heat in the attic of this creaky old building? Suddenly weary, she sighed and sat down on the step.

Then, a proverbial truth struck:

Heat rises.

✳

"By George!" Father Tim fairly whooped.

"What is it?" asked Andrew, looking up from a book on the Nativity.

"See here, sanding the surface makes this hateful color almost pleasing to the eye."

"Why, yes! I agree. It's just the color

of my good wife's pumpkin soup with a dash of cream, not bad at all. And I like the way the gilt underpainting comes forth on the sleeve."

"Do you think we can get away with sanding only? No painting?" One could dream.

"We can't know until you get at each one, but I'd say no, too easy. Let me have a go at one."

Andrew put the book down and was examining an angel as Fred came in.

"What about me sittin' in on this?" asked Fred, looking eager.

"Here's a sheet of sandpaper, pull up a chair," said Andrew. "The doorbell will tell us if we have visitors. Probably won't see a soul 'til the Charleston decorator arrives at two."

"I b'lieve I'll try a sheep. My gran'-daddy raised sheep, he let me feed th' orphans on a bottle."

"Splendid," said Father Tim. "Go to it!"

"This figure has a truly beautiful countenance," said Andrew. "What about her missing wing?"

"I don't think I'll tackle it." Truth be told, he was frightened of trying to build something so crucial with plaster, which was as yet a foreign material to him—it could result in an onerous lump instead of an arched and lovely wing. And then there were the *feathers* he'd be forced to create in the wet plaster. No indeed, this was Nativity 101, not Rodin's atelier. "Besides, think how the missing wing depicts the human condition!"

"A somewhat esoteric thought," said Andrew, pulling at his chin. "Nonetheless, I'm in!"

As the men worked with easy absorption, Father Tim smelled the fresh coffee on the hob; he heard the busy *whisk, whisk* of sandpaper, and Beethoven's "Pastorale" pouring from Andrew's radio.

He felt a happy contentment flowing up in him, as a spring from a hidden source.

When Scott called in the afternoon, Hope told him all that she was thinking. He said he'd drop by after she closed the store, if that was OK, and help out. Would she like pizza with everything, or just cheese?

As long as she could remember, she'd had it with just cheese.

"Everything!" she said, suddenly filled with unspeakable happiness.

"Well, I'll be . . ."

Avis Packard had locked up The Local and was going to his car in the alley, when he glanced north along the twilit street. It was the first time in memory that he'd seen a light above the bookstore.

As he walked Barnabas to the monument a little after nine o'clock, Father Tim noticed it, too.

He drew his wool scarf close against the chill October wind and mused how the light seemed to cheer the hushed and empty street.

Five

*T*he first Sunday of Advent dawned bitterly cold and clear beneath the platinum sheen of a half moon.

Random gusts of wind whistled around houses, rattling shutters and downspouts. Smoke was snatched from the chimneys of early risers and hurtled east by a freezing westerly blow.

At the yellow house on Wisteria Lane, Father Tim let Barnabas into the yard, and whistled him in again. Then he read the Morning Office in his study and carried two mugs of coffee upstairs, where Cynthia opened the first door on their Advent calendar.

Propped in bed against the pillows, she read aloud the supplication from the prophet Isaiah.

"'Let the sky rain down justice, and the earth bud forth a saviour!'"

"Amen!" he said, handing her a mug.

He leaned over and kissed her on the forehead. "A blessed Advent to you, beloved."

She put the palm of her hand to his cheek. "And to you, dearest."

"I've set out your little crèche."

"Oh, that ragged thing!"

"Fourteen years old, and sewing robes for those clothespins!" He recklessly counted this among the most endearing things he knew about his wife.

"Phoo, darling!"

"I want to thank you for something." He sat on her side of their bed and took a sip of the strong, black brew. "I want to thank you for encouraging me to retire."

"But you've struggled with it so."

"I know. I think most people do. But I was exhausted all the time; I never knew how to rest or take a break, or how to refuel. I think God is at last teaching me something about that."

"Hoppy said if you hadn't retired, your health would have suffered greatly."

"I wish I'd spent the last couple of years enjoying retirement instead of fighting it. But now I believe I can." He grinned. "I'm giving up the book of essays. It's a blasted nuisance."

"Hallelujah, darling! You always looked woeful when you sat down to an essay."

"I thought I had to stay busy with something important, that I had no right to rest. Of course, I want to keep myself open to any use He might make of me."

"Look at the use He's made of you in supplying so many pulpits, and the lives that were changed in that wonderful year at Whitecap, and the way you found Sammy. . . ."

"Ah, well," he said, mildly flustered. Though he had no knack for totting up such things, his wife definitely possessed a certain skill. "I have a confession to make about the essays—I've just realized it in the last few days. I thought I had to keep up, somehow, with my successful wife."

"But you don't."

"But I don't."

"I love you," she said.

"I love you back."

They were silent for a moment, comforted, as the wind keened around the north corner of the house.

"We used to talk about what we might do when I retired," he said. "You always wanted to travel. Truth be told, it's something I'm beginning to think I'd like to do."

"Your old fear of flying—is it going away?"

"A lot of my fears seem to be going away."

"Remember how I used to be afraid you'd leave me?" she asked. "That fear has vanished completely."

He raised his coffee mug in a glad salute. "After our year at Meadowgate, how would you like to go to Ireland?"

"Ireland! I'd love to go to Ireland!"

"See the Kavanagh family castle, muck about with the cousins, do rubbings of gravestones . . . like that." His heart lifted up.

She set her coffee on the bedside table and opened her arms to the man whom she'd always believed, even when others didn't suspect it, to be wise and romantic, witty and ardent, generous and brave—in the end, the truest soul she had ever known.

At the end of an unpaved road, in a white frame house surrounded by three acres of pines, Lew Boyd sat up in bed and yawned. He didn't know if he wanted to go to church this morning or not.

If he remembered right, this afternoon was the annual Advent Walk. A horde of locals would start out at the Episcopalians, then march around to the Presbyterians and Methodists, enjoying a brief service at each stop and singing hymns and carols along the way. The whole caboodle would end up at First Baptist, with all the hot cider, cookies, and whatnot a man could hold.

If he showed up at church this morning, the elders would be after him to join the walkers this afternoon and fill in the bass. You'd think a town church, especially Baptist, would have more than one poor rube to sing bass, but no deal—it was his luck to be the spotted monkey. Over and over again, they'd tried to trick him into joining the choir in order to regulate his churchgoing, but even he wasn't dumb enough to go for that stunt.

In the great commotion outside, he heard his garbage can slam against the side of the house.

A man couldn't sing bass in gale-force winds and freezing temperatures! Besides, he'd just worked six days at a hard run; why would he want to go walking? Come to think of it, now that he had cable, he ought to just hole up at home and get it over with. Of course, Earlene would be asking if he was going to church. . . .

He checked his Timex. About now, she'd be taking her mama's little dab of breakfast up the stairs and fluffing the pillows so her mama could sit up in bed and eat, with Earlene feeding her every bite. Then, in a little bit, the next-door neighbor would come over and Earlene would go off to church, looking pretty as a speckled pup and toting the chess pie she'd baked last night for the Coffee Minute.

That's the way Earlene was, she cared about people. Nearly forty-five years ago, when he'd won a blue ribbon in that pickle contest, Earlene had run over and kissed him, then run off, embarrassed half to death by what she'd done.

He'd never forgotten that moment, even when he was married to Juanita.

"Why'd you do that?" he asked when he and Earlene met again a few years ago. "I didn't even hardly know you."

"I didn't know I was goin' to do it 'til I *did* it!" she said, blushing. "I secretly liked you, and I just felt so . . . *happy* 'cause you'd won!"

In his heart, he was sometimes hard on Earlene for not being here. But he was disgusted with himself for this. She didn't deserve it. Taking care of her failing mama was what she'd committed to do; plus, she wanted to work another few months at the flour company to get her retirement benefits—she'd told him right up front that this is how it would be, and he'd accepted it and married her.

Then there were her sisters, who said if the word leaked out that they were married, it would kill her mama. Lord knows, he didn't want to be party to a thing like that, no way. Except for telling Father Tim, he'd kept the whole blooming thing a secret. He knew as well as anybody that news travels—it'd run straight up to Knoxville on both legs, hard as it could go.

Next weekend, he'd take Saturday off and go see her. He'd stay with his old Aunt Bess, as usual, and do a few odd jobs for his elderly relative, like fix her top porch step and put a new shelf in her pantry.

In the evening, Earlene's neighbor would come in to sit, and he'd take his bride out to a nice dinner, maybe surf and turf. He felt a little shiver of happiness as he imagined helping her up in his new truck, and giving her a big kiss.

They'd hold hands and sit together on the same side of the booth, and he'd try not to say a word about how hard it was to keep living like this. And he dern sure wouldn't say, like he'd said one time before, Well, sugar, how long do you think it'll take your little mama to die?

Nossir, he'd never do that again. He should've been strung up by his feet.

He sniffed the cold air of the bedroom. The new coffeemaker with the timer had kicked on in the kitchen.

After drinking two mugs of engine oil and knocking back a couple of Pop-Tarts, maybe he'd spend the day laid up in bed watching the Titans shut down the New York Giants.

Whop. The garbage can slammed against the porch rail.

"Go, Titans!" he hollered.

Around ten o'clock, the winds increased; leaves that had fallen during a hard November rain were blown upon the sharp, clean air like coveys of startled quail.

On Main Street, a red scarf was snatched from the shoulders of a churchgoer and hurled aloft, dipping and tossing like a Chinese kite, before it landed on the green awning of Sweet Stuff Bakery.

The Kavanaghs observed the wonderment of the flying scarf as they drove to Wesley for the ten o'clock service at St. Paul's.

"It definitely won't be an Advent Walk," said Cynthia. "More like an Advent *Run!*"

"I may leave the walk a mite early this afternoon."

"Really?"

"And I may be a tad late for dinner."

"Whatever for?"

He smiled, his eyes on the road. "Christmas is coming, you know."

She looked at him, beaming. "Of course, dearest! That explains everything!"

"Come, thou long expected Jesus,
Born to set thy people free;

From our fears and sins release us,
Let us find our rest in Thee.
Israel's strength and consolation,
Hope of all the earth Thou art;
Dear desire of every nation,
Joy of every longing heart. . . ."

The walkers sang lustily as they processed from an inspiring service at the Methodist chapel and turned north on Main Street. They were hard by the fire station when Lew Boyd saw Father Tim weaving his way quickly through the procession, moving south.

"You're goin' th' wrong way!" hollered Lew, in case the Father didn't know they were headed back to First Baptist for hot cider and all the trimmings.

"A blessed Advent!" shouted Father Tim. He raised a gloved hand in salute and kept going, the wind at his back.

From the window above Happy Endings, Hope Winchester peered down
upon the straggle of walkers making
their way to First Baptist while holding
on for dear life to their sheet music.

> *"Lift up your heads, ye mighty gates;*
> *Behold, the King of glory waits;*
> *The King of kings is drawing near;*
> *The Savior of the world is here! . . .*
> *Fling wide the portals of your heart;*
> *Make it a temple, set apart . . ."*

She was happy that she could hear
most of the words, liking especially
"Fling wide the portals of your heart."

In the music floating up to her, she
was struck by a deep, resonant voice
that was clearly able to bind the other
voices together. She looked for its
source, but couldn't locate it, and was
turning away from the window when
someone peered up at her and waved.

She waved back, glad to be noticed,

and stood and watched the toboggans and flapping coattails disappear beneath the green awning.

She turned to go downstairs, but stopped instead and gazed at the large room, now delivered of the detritus of more than two decades. It was empty, clean, and bright with the dazzle of winter light.

It had been six long weeks since she'd sent the letter, but she hadn't heard a word from Mrs. Mallory. Possibly she intended to lease the building to someone else and hadn't informed her, nor did Helen know anything. If Helen's movers had to come and take everything away, the packing needed to begin at once; only the stock she was conserving for Christmas sales could wait until the last minute.

Then there was the letter to her landlady, who would need to know something immediately. . . .

She found she was wringing her

hands, a habit she had tried without success to break.

But, no! She would not give up.

Even with concerns that sometimes overwhelmed her, she refused to abandon her belief in a glad outcome.

Don't worry about anything, Hope, Father Tim had said, *but in everything, by prayer and supplication, with thanksgiving . . .*

"'. . . make your requests known unto God,'" she recited aloud, going quickly down the stairs, "'and the peace that passes all understanding will fill your heart and mind through Christ Jesus!'"

Finding Margaret Ann at her feet, she picked her up and held her close and stroked her orange fur.

She would have to let her secret out to Mrs. Havner. She would go and speak with her at once . . .

. . . then she would call Louise and say she might be moving home to live with her in their mother's house, with its overgrown garden of hollyhocks and foxglove . . .

. . . and she would call Scott and ask if he would come for spaghetti and meat-balls this evening—it was the only dish she knew how to make for com-pany. . . .

Her heart skipped a beat at the thought of cooking for Scott and set-ting the table for the two of them. With everything else before her, it was al-most too much even to consider, but she remembered how she would feel in his company—she would feel happy and unafraid.

She stopped for a moment, leaning against the newel-post at the foot of the stairs; Margaret Ann's rhythmic purr resonated upon her heart. Though she and Helen hadn't discussed it, they both knew that Margaret Ann would find a new home with Hope.

Whatever happens, she thought, I must continue to believe in a glad outcome—but I must also prepare for whatever else may lie ahead.

She suddenly felt purposeful, and relieved, as if a great weight had flown from her shoulders.

"I'm makin' a list and checkin' it twice," said Fred.

Fred had volunteered to give him a hand today, an offer that might not be valid any other Sunday this month.

"You've got your five sheep, you've got your donkey, and you've got your first shepherd knocked out," said Fred. "That's seven down an' a dozen or so to go."

All sanding and priming was done, and the seven finished pieces stood lined up on a shelf above the sink.

"Hallelujah!" said Father Tim, slipping into a green bib apron. "Ol' time, it is a-flyin'!" He hadn't made the deadline to put the shepherds and all the sheep on the sideboard today. Now the plan was to set out the complete scene on Christmas Eve.

Freshly ground coffee dripped into the pot; two slices of pumpkin pie, as frozen as bricks since Thanksgiving dinner at the yellow house, sat thawing on the drain board of the sink.

"You got four ewes an' a ram to go. You want me to keep doin' sheep?"

"Keep doing sheep!" said Father Tim. "And God bless you for it!" He rolled up his sleeves and sat down at his worktable across from Fred. "For several years, it seemed that every Christmas season, the Lord would send me a Christmas angel, somebody who came along at just the right time, to give me a hand or help me over a hurdle. I believe you're my Christmas angel this year, and I thank you."

Fred ducked his head, shy. "An' I thank you, Father, for lettin' me sit in on this. My wife's glad to get me out of th' house. She's got two quilts to get done."

"Would you call me Tim?"

"Nossir, I can't do that."

"Why not?"

"I never call a preacher by a first name."

"Does this mean I have to call you Mr. Addison?"

Fred laughed. "Nossir, that's what the IRS called me last spring, an' I've had a dislike for th' sound of it ever since."

"What would I do if I had to stipple this whole flock?" Father Tim threw up his hands. "I'd be here 'til lambing time!"

"I like stipplin', but I wouldn't want to fool with *wings* or *robes*—and 'specially wouldn't want to fool with *skin;* nossir, you're th' Skin Man. Look at that shepherd on th' shelf! Real as life!"

And, by heaven, it was. Father Tim was amazed that the shepherd had started out with a horrific case of jaundice and now looked merely well tanned, which would certainly be expected in his line of work.

The damaged hand, however, had been another matter. He and Fred and Andrew had all had a go at it, and the effort-by-committee showed. But there was no looking back. The hand was done, they were not Michelangelos around here.

Father Tim took the second shepherd from the shelf and examined it, turning it in his hands. "I think I'll start with the robe—any ideas?"

Fred scratched his head. "Seems like shepherds would've stayed pretty ragged-lookin.' I reckon they slept under bushes or rocks or like that."

"Actually, shepherds around Bethlehem lived in caves. Caves made safe places for their flocks at night."

"Maybe somethin' th' color of a burlap sack?"

"That might be hard." He took a deep breath. "But let me see what I can do."

He squeezed a bit of paint from three tubes into a saucer and blended the col-

ors with a plastic knife. He wanted to
get his fingers in the stuff, but the tell-
tale signs of oil glaze were hard to remove, and harder still to hide from an
inquisitive wife.

He showed the contents of the saucer
to Fred. "What do you think?"

"You goin' for burlap?"

"Going for burlap."

"I'd say a little more brown."

"Done!"

They worked for a time, silent, obliv-
ious to the Mozart concerto on the
radio.

"These tails are way yonder longer'n
we used to do at my gran'daddy's. We
docked 'em pretty short when I was
comin' along."

"How many sheep did you have?"

"Four hundred!"

"Man!" he said, quoting Dooley.

"We raised Dorset, mostly, and a few
Blue Face. I was what you might call a
shepherd, myself, now an' again."

Father Tim figured he'd been seven

or eight years old the Christmas he determined to do what the Bethlehem
shepherds had done.

Reverend Simon, a fervent Bible
scholar and his mother's much-loved
Baptist preacher, explained the passage
from Luke to the Sunday School class
of eight- to ten-year-olds. Reverend
Simon had them all toeing the mark; he
was a big man with unruly hair and
spectacles that enlarged his eyes in a
frightening way. Someone said he had
ruined his eyes reading the Bible, and
knew more about everything in it than
anyone alive. He taught their class the
way he taught the congregation, with
extravagant gestures and studied pauses
and bursts of song in a rich, baritone
voice that rattled the windowpanes.

"Who were these shepherds?" he
thundered. His magnified brown eyes
roamed the small classroom as if demanding an answer, but no one raised a
hand.

"They were merely a few local boys

from over the hill! Boys like you, Tom, and you, Chester, and you, Timothy!

"When they received the word from the heavenly host and recovered from their fright, what did they do? They didn't dillydally, they didn't put it off 'til morning, they didn't wait 'til they'd fried up some bacon, they made *haste!* 'And they came with *haste,*' St. Luke tells us, they came *lickety-split* toward that bright and shining star, to see the wonder of the Savior, to experience His glory, to observe His mystery.

"Now, children, how do you think they got there?"

Though Reverend Simon had no intention of soliciting an answer, Mary Jane Mason raised her hand with fear and trembling, and replied with the only transport known to her. "In a Dodge sedan?"

"My dear child, they had no Dodge sedan nor even a Buick Town Car, they had no mules or oxen or donkeys or carts or wagons. Indeed, they had no mode of transport save their own two *feet!*"

Reverend Simon lifted one exceedingly large foot, shod in a shoe as black as a washpot, to demonstrate.

"Indeed, they would have *trod* the several miles to the inn, almost certainly *barefoot* . . ."

Here, Reverend Simon shivered mightily, wrapped an imaginary cloak about his large frame, and peered at them over his spectacles. ". . . and in the *bristling cold* . . ."

A long pause as he looked around at them.

". . . in the *bristling* cold of a *dark* and *wintry* night!"

Wishing to move beyond the carved and static figures of their Nativity scene, and enter somehow into the miracle itself, he had asked Tommy to walk around the barn with him the night before Christmas. He was convinced that something as fraught with risk and danger as this would responsibly equal the shepherds' longer trek to the inn.

"I ain't walkin' around no barn at night," said Tommy. "An' I 'specially ain't doin' it barefooted."

"But the shepherds had to do it, they had to walk all the way from the sheep pasture to Bethlehem while it was *pitch-black dark.*"

"I ain't doin' it," said Tommy.

He had screwed up his courage then and, after donning an old sheet tied at his waist by a piece of jump rope, sat on the top porch step and waited for nightfall. He had checked the feet of the shepherds in their Nativity scene, and, to his enormous relief, they were wearing shoes.

On her way home to the little house down the road, Peggy stopped on the porch and patted his head. "Your mama say come back soon as you does this."

He nodded.

At the foot of the steps, she turned and looked at him. "An' don't you be lettin' any spooks git my baby."

He had heard that, on Christmas Eve, animals talked, which seemed spooky enough. He wondered if he'd hear their two cows talking in the barn. The thought gave him a funny feeling in his stomach; he couldn't imagine cows talking or what they might say. What if they busted out talking while he was down there by himself, in the dark?

His mouth had been dry with fear, yet he wanted more than anything to somehow be one with those privileged to be first.

"What are you doing?" His father approached the foot of the steps, seemingly annoyed to find his son wearing a sheet over his clothes and, worse still, accomplishing nothing of consequence.

"I'm going to walk around the barn when it gets dark." He said this louder than he might have done. "Sir."

His father looked at him as he often did—without appearing to see him.

"Like the shepherds," he said, eager to explain, and thereby make himself seen.

"The shepherds?"

"That went to worship the Baby Jesus. I know they didn't walk around the barn, but . . ."

In the leaden winter sky, a star or two had already appeared, and a sliver of moon. A bird called somewhere by the rabbit pen.

"Timothy . . ."

Something in his father's voice was suddenly different; his eyes shone with a tenderness his son had never seen before.

His father gazed at him for an instant more, then walked up the steps and into the house.

He had sat there, numb with a mixture of joy and bewilderment. In one brief and startling moment, he realized that he was, after all, seen—and perhaps even loved. His heart beat faster, and his breath nearly left him.

As dusk faded toward nightfall, he prayed again and walked down the steps onto frozen grass that crackled beneath his shoes like dry leaves.

More stars had appeared; he looked above the ridge of the barn roof and picked a bright star that he might follow.

He had reached the barn and touched its silvery, unpainted wood when he heard footsteps behind him. He whirled around and, in the twilit gloom, saw the figure of his father.

"Timothy . . ."

His father had walked with him then, neither of them speaking. When he, Timothy, stumbled over a castaway bucket, he instinctively flung out his hand, and his father caught it and held it in his own, and, in the cold and velveteen darkness, they continued around the silent barn, toward the house in which every window gleamed with light.

"This pie's thawed," said Fred, sticking his forefinger into the filling.

"I'm sorry—what did you say?"

Timothy . . . The memory of that single and astonishing connection with his father might be lost for years at a time, only to return when least expected. . . .

"Pie's thawed. You want coffee?"

"Sure," he said, hoarse with feeling.

He walked home along the empty sidewalk, illumined by a choir of angels. Formed by hundreds of tiny lights, the angels gleamed from every lamppost on both sides of their modest Main Street, giving it the look of a large and gracious boulevard.

Gouging funds out of the town budget for a host of angels had, in his opinion, been the finest hour of their former mayor, Esther Cunningham.

"You've been scarce as hens' teeth," said Mule.

"Busy," said Father Tim, thumping into the rear booth.

"Big deal. Everybody's busy this time of year. I've been havin' to do breakfast and lunch solo."

"What's J.C. doing? Starving to death?"

"We had lunch at th' tea shop yesterday, and breakfast th' day before."

"You just said you'd been eating solo."

Mule grinned. "I said that to make you feel sorry for me."

"It isn't working."

Father Tim opened the single-fold menu. He was up for something different today. Enough already with tuna on dry toast.

"Tell you what," said Mule, "I'll let you order for me! How's that? You know what I like—order me whatever you want to!"

"I can't order for you, buddyroe, you can't even order for yourself."

Mule shrugged. "I don't have a clue what I want."

"There's the rub." As for himself, maybe he'd try the taco salad. Or the pimiento cheese on whole wheat . . .

"I guess you heard what's movin' into this buildin' when Percy leaves."

"Nope. I've been out of the loop for a while."

"A shoe store!"

"Great news!"

"That's what I said. A man shouldn't have to drive to another town to buy shoes."

"You don't drive to another town to buy shoes," said Father Tim. "All your shoes come from yard sales in Mitford."

"A penny saved is a penny earned. So what am I havin'?" Mule leaned forward in anticipation, as Velma swooped over like a crow from a pine tree.

"Let me tell 'im what he's havin'!" She shot her glasses down her nose, meaning business; she didn't have all day to yank an order out of Mule Skinner. "He's havin' a bowl of vegetable soup with a hot cornstick! Today's special!"

Mule gave Velma a dark look. "What's in th' vegetable soup?"

"Vegetables," she said, tight-lipped.

"Wait. Whoa." Father Tim knew where this was headed. "Bring him a bacon cheeseburger, everything but onions, with fries on the side and a Diet Coke. And . . ." Should he do this?

"And . . . ?" Velma's pencil was poised in the air.

"And I'll have the same!" He exhaled.

Speechless, Velma adjusted her glasses and stumped away.

"Did you know," said Father Tim,

"that the average American eats over sixteen pounds of fries per year? As I've had only two or three orders in the last decade, I figure I'm due roughly a hundred and fifty-nine pounds."

"There's only one problem," said Mule.

"What's that?"

"Th' grease Percy uses for fries is th' same he uses for fish. I don't much like fish."

"So I've been wondering—how is J.C. getting upstairs to his pressroom since he refuses to set foot in this place?"

"He's usin' th' window on th' landin'."

"There's more than one way to skin a cat."

"Just shoots up th' bottom sash, slips in like a house burglar, and up th' steps he goes. By th' way . . ."

He thought Mule looked pained. "Yes?"

"Fancy don't like me to eat bacon."

"I forgot to ask Percy who won the photo contest. Did you hear?"

"Lew Boyd."

"Great. That was a good shot."

"Plus . . . ," said Mule.

"Plus what?"

"Plus Fancy wants me to cut out cheese. Too constipatin'."

"So! If you could have anything you want, what would you like for Christmas?"

"Anything I want? Price no object?"

"Right."

"A Rolodex watch!"

"Aha!" said Father Tim, as their orders arrived with more than the usual flourish.

✴

He was glad Cynthia was out to a tea at Olivia Harper's when Dooley called.

"Hey," said Dooley.

"Hey, yourself, buddyroe! What's up? When are you headed home?"

"December twentieth."

"We can't wait. I'll have something to show you, but you mustn't tell Cynthia."

"I won't, I promise."

"I'm working on an old Nativity scene—twenty-odd pieces! Angels, shepherds, wise men, sheep—we've got ten sheep, total, a whole flock!"

"You sound excited."

"I am. It's great. Wait 'til you see it. I'm painting shepherds now. Next come angels."

"Sounds hard."

"It is hard." He realized he was grinning. "But it's . . ." He thought a moment. "It's *fun.*"

"So save me somethin' to paint," said Dooley.

"Are you kidding?"

"No, I'm serious."

"Consider it done! Have you heard from Sammy?"

"He wrote me a letter. I'll bring it so you and Cynthia can read it. It meant a lot to him to be with everybody at Thanksgiving."

"Buck and I are going down to see him next week." Buck Leeper was Dooley's stepdad, and a zealous teammate in the search for Dooley's siblings. "We'll take Poo and Jessie. I hope Sammy will come for Christmas."

"That would be great." Dooley sounded pensive. "I've been thinking—would you take him all the clothes in my closet except my green sweatshirt and the last pair of jeans Cynthia bought me?"

"He's a little taller than you, but we'll give it a try."

"Umm, don't take that Italian suit Cynthia made me wear in New York, or the belt that's hanging on the door."

"Got it."

There was a brief silence.

"Dad?"

"Yes?"

"Do you think—I mean, like, really—that we'll ever find Kenny?"

"Yes!" he said without hesitating. "Yes!"

"You haven't given up?"

"Never! I don't know what to do right now, but God has been faithful. Four out of five, son! Let's keep thanking Him for His providence ... and praying and believing He'll lead us to Kenny. Is that a deal?"

"Yes, sir," said Dooley. "It's a deal."

"I've been thinking," he said, taking her hand.

They lay in bed and looked up at the ceiling, at the place where the streetlamp shone in and cast its light.

"Tell me," she said.

"All these years, I've remembered the hard things about my father. His indifference to my mother, his coldness toward me, his rage, his depression, the countless times he hurt us."

"Yes," she whispered.

"When a person spends a lifetime

hurting himself and others, it's hard to remember the good things about him."

"Yes. I know."

"I want to start remembering the time he looked at me . . ." His voice broke, and he lay still for a time. "It was only a look, nothing more, but it said everything I'd ever hoped to know."

There was a long silence.

"And then he walked around the barn with me." He couldn't stop the flow of tears, nor did he wish to.

"Tell me about it, dearest."

He told her.

With all his heart, and with all his soul, he would attempt to put that moment, that dark yet somehow shining hour, at the front of his memories about his father. After all these years, it would be enough.

At last, it would be enough.

Six

*F*ather Tim opened the fifteenth door of their Advent calendar and read aloud a brief exegesis of verses from Luke's second chapter.

"'And Joseph went up from Nazareth to Bethlehem, to be enrolled with Mary, who was with child.'"

Cynthia thumbed the pages of her Bible to a map of the region that extended south from the Sea of Galilee. "From Galilee in the north to Judea in the south seems a long way, Timothy."

"Maybe ninety to a hundred miles. On a donkey, that's roughly a week's travel. It could have taken longer, of course, because of the pregnancy."

"I wonder what they ate."

"Whatever it was, they probably

bought it from camel trains. They couldn't have carried many supplies."

"Isn't a lot of this terrain open desert?"

"It is."

"What would the weather have been like?"

"Cold. Very cold," he said. "Some say too cold for the shepherds around Bethlehem to be in the fields. They would have had their flocks under cover by October or November."

"So the birth may have occurred earlier, before they left the fields?"

"Very likely. However, the tradition of a late-December Nativity is eighteen centuries old, and I'm not messing with that."

"Still, if they were traveling in December, nighttime temperatures would have been freezing." His wife pondered this, shaking her head. "Just think! All that misery over *taxes!*"

"Some things," he said, "never change."

Harold Newland, the postman, bolted through the door at Happy Endings with a bundle of mail secured by a rubber band.

"That's a load off!" he said, thumping it on the counter next to Margaret Ann.

"How about a cup of hot cider?" Hope thought Harold looked worn, to say the least. Probably all the catalogs, plus the fact that his wife, Emma, was in Atlanta with her pregnant daughter until after Christmas. . . .

"No time to lollygag!" he said, hitching up his belt. "Have a good day!"

"'Thanks, and thanks, and ever thanks!'" Hope exclaimed, quoting Shakespeare.

The postcard was on top. She saw it at once.

Margaret Ann eyed Harold's departure as Hope withdrew the card from beneath the rubber band and turned it over. It was from George Gaynor, known to Mitford as the Man in the Attic. After eight years in prison and a brief job assignment at Happy Endings, he had returned to the prison system as a chaplain.

Inscribed in a bold hand, the card read:

Dear Hope,
Keep living up to your name.
Your brother in Christ,
George

She blinked to hold back the tears. She was trying to live up to her name, but it was growing harder each day.

It was now December 15, and still she'd had no word from Mrs. Mallory. Helen had phoned the Mallory attorneys on her behalf, but they claimed to know nothing about their client's plans for this particular property, which was one of many in Mitford, Florida, and Spain.

She walked to the window facing Main Street. Though the future seemed as dark as the lowering sky above the town, she would try to hold fast to what was positive and bright.

Holiday sales had been wonderful, she couldn't complain, and Helen was hoping with her that Happy Endings might remain in Mitford.

Father Tim now knew her secret, which was a source of great relief. He had prayed with her and agreed to compose a letter of reference to Edith Mallory, so it would be ready when needed. She was touched that he said "when" and not "if."

Though many circumstances were positive, she was, nonetheless, exhausted. The rare-book business on the Internet, coupled with "running the floor," as Helen would say, had taken a toll. She was bitterly tired at the end of the day, and often slept fitfully. Helen had sharply reminded her that things wouldn't get better if the shop became hers. "Quite the contrary," Helen had said. And when would she be able to afford help?

Indeed, she had never wanted to be "management" until the day God had given her the amazing idea of actually owning the shop.

She found herself wringing her hands pitiably, and dropped them to her sides at once. How quickly she went from high to low! She must think of the lovely aspects, the glad outcome, as she'd learned from her reading in Philippians last night.

". . . whatsoever things are true, whatsoever things are honest, whatsoever things are just, whatsoever things are pure, whatsoever things are lovely . . . think on these things."

Best of all, best of anything, she would see Scott this evening. He would come directly from work, and in the empty room above the bookstore, they were going to put up a tree and decorate it with strings of colored lights.

Afterward, they'd cross the street together and look up to the middle window where it would stand, luminous and shining, for all the village to see.

Uncle Billy Watson shuffled from one end of the kitchen to the other, holding on to the stove, then to the countertop, then the table.

Here he was pacin' th' floor, and him a man hardly able t' walk in th' first dadjing place! An' where was 'is cane? How could he lose 'is cane if he hadn't left th' house?

He had two weeks t' come up with Rose's present, an' not one blessed notion had passed through his wore-out brain. Nary a one!

Over th' years, he'd growed plenty tired of hearin' what Rose's brother, Willard, had give 'er.

Before Willard died in th' war in France, he'd give 'er a dolly, he'd give 'er dresses with lace an' smockin', he'd give 'er a coat with a rabbit-fur collar, he'd give 'er a little cart an' a goat t' pull it, on an' on 'til a man could heave 'is dinner, an' then, don't you know, Willard had give 'er this *house* they was a-livin' in, an' ever' stick of furnishin'.

If he was t' miss givin' Rose a present this Christmas, hit'd be th' first time in more'n fifty years. Nossir, b'fore he'd let that happen, he'd go down th' street and buy somethin' off of a store shelf.

He remembered th' one year he'd store-bought Rose's present; th' Preacher Kavanagh had gone with 'im an' helped buy 'er a winter coat f'r half off, an' a pair of red high-heel shoes. Rose had took a fit over them shoes, but she never put 'em on 'er feet. They was still settin' out on th' mantel in their bedroom, as decoration.

He didn't recall if he had any twenties still hid in th' stacks of newspaper in th' dinin' room. Maybe one or two, he didn't rightly know. . . .

"Bill Watson! Why are you wearing out our good linoleum?" His wife stood at the kitchen door in her chenille robe, with a headful of curlers. He hadn't seen 'er in them things in a hundred years. She looked like a porkypine.

"I'm tryin' to figure out somethin' in m' *brain!*" He hollered good 'n' loud, so she'd be sure an' hear.

"You say I'm a *pain?*"

"Yessir, you are, but *that ain't what I said!*"

"Speak up, Bill Watson! *What'd you say?*"

"I said I'm tryin' t' *figure out y'r Santy Claus!*"

"My Santy Claus? Did you say my *Santy Claus?*" His wife's face lit up like a Christmas tree—she was grinnin' like a young 'un, which was a wonder he hadn't seen in a coon's age.

"Them was my words, all right!"

"Why, Bill Watson!" She trotted over an' kissed 'im on th' cheek s' hard he near about tumbled over back'ards. "That's the best news in this whole wide world!"

He was throwing caution to the winds, he was picking up speed, he was flying.

I can do this! he thought, astonished. I can do this! He was no Rembrandt, but he could turn a lurid, sallow skin into something believable, and while his donkey ear was nothing to write home about, it had a certain . . . élan.

The start-up had been slow and time-consuming, boggled by everything from five days of flu to complete ignorance about what to do and how to do it. Now, by George, he had momentum!

Not only was it a liberating thing to have, it had come in the nick of time. With less than five days remaining before Dooley's visit, and less than ten until Christmas, he and his erstwhile helpers had many a mile to go.

He found he was taking the work to bed with him, so to speak, and having trouble sleeping. Then, after hours of staring at the ceiling and planning his next move, he could hardly wait to roll into the Oxford next morning.

Some of his excitement came, perhaps, from working with his hands. Aside from gardening and cooking, it was a completely fresh experience for someone who'd always gone at life with his head. Whatever it was, he hadn't felt so energized in years.

Truth be told, while he passionately loved celebrating the liturgy, he'd nearly always dreaded coming up with a fit and useful sermon—he seemed to invest a disproportionate amount of time in woolgathering, pacing the floor, beseeching God, and laboring to have his words expound the Scriptures. Then, on the days the Holy Spirit seemed to abandon him to his own devices, there was the delivering of said words to expectant souls who needed, and deserved, more nourishment than he felt capable of giving.

He wondered if he should feel a little guilty these days about—to put it plainly—having so much fun.

His wife was in bed, pretending to read but surveying him oddly as he sat in the wing chair pretending to do the same.

He was pretending because he couldn't keep his mind on the book; he was thinking about the angel with the missing wing. He'd taken the color of her outer robe from a painting by Adolphe-William Bouguereau; he'd mixed and mixed the paints until he got something that gained a consensus in the back room.

"That's it!" Andrew exclaimed.

"Bull's-eye!" said his chief stippler.

Though white was definitely the color of choice for wings, he had found the white alone to be stark and cold, in need of subtlety. But he'd carried things too far; he had tried too hard to be subtle. He'd like to go back and glaze the wing again. . . .

He'd relished working on this particular figure, liking the way the missing wing gave the piece a whole other balance in his hands. He also loved the exquisite serenity of her countenance—he thought the maker had done a thumping good job.

The only thing was, he didn't have time to turn back and fiddle with small details, he needed to keep moving forward. . . .

"Sweetheart?"

"Speak, Kavanagh!"

"I'm about to bust."

He looked up. "Whatever for?"

"To know what you're up to." She tilted her head to one side and gazed at him, smiling. "You know I love surprises, but really, Timothy, I don't think I can *make* it 'til Christmas."

"Get over it, girl, you'll gouge nothing out of me."

"All that paint on the pants you stuck behind the boiler in the basement . . ."

"You've been snooping behind the boiler in the basement?"

"Yes, Father, I confess."

"Aha." He went back to his book. *Blast!*

"And on your hands, of course."

"What about my hands?" Didn't he scrub them diligently to remove all traces?

"I can smell it, dear. Oil paint gets into the pores. You're painting something!"

What could he say? "Curiosity killed the cat!"

When he walked Barnabas to the monument at nine o'clock, he saw the tree glittering in the window above the bookstore. Colored light spilled over the awning and reflected on the rain-wet pavement.

In the face of losing everything one hoped for, lighting a tree was an act of faith. Well done! he thought, pulling his hat down and his collar up.

He walked more briskly, glad to be alive on the hushed and lamplit street where every storefront gleamed with promise.

"'And there were in that same country . . . ,'" said his mother.

"'Shepherds abiding!'"

"Very good, dear. And where were they abiding?"

"'In the field!'"

"And what were they doing?"

"'Keeping watch o'er their flock by night!'"

"Yes!" said his mother, pleased. He liked pleasing his mother, for he loved her more than anything, even more than Peggy. He also liked saying "o'er" instead of "over."

His mother had spent hours teaching him the story of Christ's birth, and the images she instilled in him had been vivid and thrilling, like a kind of movie cast with a score of animals—the great camels plowing over the desert sands, the donkey on which the Virgin Mary probably rode with Joseph walking beside her, the sheep and cows and horses in the hay-scented stable. . . .

And then, to top it all off, there was the heavenly host.

When as a child he heard the passages from Luke read aloud, he had also, on two separate occasions, heard the proclamation delivered by a multitude of voices. Though Scripture said nothing about the proclamation being sung, he was convinced otherwise—in truth, the music had come to him in the region of his heart as well as his mind, and the sound of the great chorale had been beautiful beyond all imagining.

Of course, he wouldn't have told anyone that he'd heard—as if in his own sky, above his own house—*Glory to God in the highest, and on earth peace, good will toward men. . . .*

He'd resigned himself even then to a simple fact: there were things he could never share with another, granting the occasional exception of his mother, who, more than anyone, believed him to speak from a true heart.

Indeed, there was no denying he'd been an often lonely and wildly imaginative child, but he was glad of it; for many things that deserved to be believed, he had believed with all his might.

Here he was with his nose stuck in a book at six o'clock in the evening, under a bare bulb in the back room of the Oxford. He hadn't meant this thing to devour his every waking moment. . . .

It was all the robes and undergarments that had him out on a limb. Now that he had eyes to see, there seemed to be a thousand folds needing light and shadow. All along, he'd been painting the clothing without light and shadow, knowing that something was wrong, but what?

Blast. What if he packed up the whole business and stored it in the attic until another time? But he knew the answer to that—there would never be another time.

Possibly all that was needed was a kind of smudge that followed the line of a fold—something darker than the garment, yet something simple.

With the book open beside him on the worktable, he mixed a daub of paint and, without thinking, put it on his thumb and worked the color along the left side of the fold of the angel's robe, then retraced the line with his forefinger and gently smoothed away some of the color.

Ahhhh . . .

There!
Thank you, Lord. . . .
Done.

The pain had moved into the region of her heart and seemed lodged there like a stickpin.

In case the letter had gone astray, she had rewritten it from memory and sent it again, this time declaring it urgent that Mrs. Mallory respond as quickly as possible.

Mrs. Havner had said she could take her time about the apartment.

"You've been a fine tenant," she said, "and for you, I'll forget the two weeks' notice. Just let me know when you know." Mrs. Havner had given her a little pan of warm gingerbread and a hug. She wanted to cling there on her landlady's broad and cushioned shoulder, and weep like a child.

With the exception of what she would need until she moved, every-

thing in the apartment was packed. After all, whether she moved only a few
doors down the street or home to live
with Louise, the packing must be done.

In truth, she was beginning to know
it would be her mother's old home,
that this was what God must want for
her. Anyone could see that if Mrs. Mallory were going to let her have the
building, she would have been notified
by now.

In the short months since she prayed
that prayer with George Gaynor, she
hadn't yet found how to hold on to
God's peace. Sometimes, as she prayed,
it would come to her like a bird flying
in at the window; it would settle on her
shoulder, and she would feel trans-
ported by relief and glad expectation.
Then the anxiety would flood in, and
the startled bird would fly away. . . .

But no matter what happened,
Christmas sales were booming. She'd
had the biggest order ever, from Olivia
Harper, and knew she could count on

something sizable from Father Tim and Cynthia. . . .

The bell on the door jangled as four Mitford schoolteachers tumbled in, laughing, their cheeks glowing from the sharp, bright cold. She had opened an hour and a half early so they could shop before the last day of school began.

"Would you like a cup of hot cider?"

"Oh, yes!" said Miss Griggs of first grade. "We'd like that better than anything!"

Emily Townsend of third grade unwound the candy-striped muffler from her neck. "Your tree is really special. It kind of gives me . . . *goose bumps* when Charlie and I ride by at night. It seems so . . . *consoling,* somehow. . . . I don't know how to express it—Sharon is the one who loves English! Oh, and here are some cookies I made. I hope you like pecans, we cracked them ourselves—can you *believe* it, they are *so* hard to pick out of the shell!"

"Oh, my!" said Hope, admiring the large cookies.

Miss Wilson, also of third grade, removed her red earmuffs. "We *all* love the tree in your upstairs window, it's very *cheering.*"

"Thank you!" Hope realized she felt considerably cheered herself.

"Is it true you're going to have story time all summer?"

A heavy weight came upon her heart. What could she say? "That," she managed, "is my fondest desire." Please, God, she thought.

He arrived at the Oxford a few minutes before Andrew or Fred and, having his own key, let himself into the darkened room that smelled of beeswax and old wood.

He'd always loved the scent of the Oxford, but had grown fonder still of its rich and varied odors. Even the smell of the oil-based materials used for the figures had become welcome and familiar, quickening his senses as ink must do for someone in the printing trade.

He switched on the light and looked at the long shelf above the sink. Next to the camel, which he was saving for Dooley's expertise, he had lined up the finished figures.

Nine ewes, a ram, two angels, a donkey!

Three wise men, two shepherds . . .

They were coming up on the Holy Family.

He was pulling off his coat and scarf when he heard Fred unlock the front door and step inside, apparently with someone else.

"I saw th' Father turn in here about five minutes ago. I need to see 'im!"

"I wouldn't go back there," said Fred.

Father Tim hurried from the back room to find Mule charging his way.

"There you are!" said Mule. "I got a predicament!"

Father Tim stood firm by a Georgian

dining table, blocking further passage; Mule wasn't much, after all, on keeping secrets.

"J.C. wants you an' me to have lunch at th' tea shop today, but I been thinkin'. Ol' Percy's goin' to be out of there in a few days, and seems like to eat at th' tea shop right now would be really disrespectful."

"I think you're dead right."

"I ate there two days last week, but I didn't feel good about it."

"Tell J.C. we'll catch him at the tea shop after the Grill closes."

"He'll be sore."

"He'll get over it."

"So what're you hangin' out down here for? Somebody said you come in here every day now."

"I'm working on a special project."

"Doin' what?"

"A little of this, a little of that. You know."

"Right," said Mule.

"So," said Father Tim, "I've got to get cracking. See you at the Grill? The usual time?"

Mule looked doleful. "I wish J.C. hadn't blown up at Velma right before th' holidays, what with Percy closin' an' all."

"Me, too."

When Mule was safely out the door, he trotted to the back room to grind the coffee. Fresh Antigua, six heaping scoops, four of decaf, two of the hard stuff.

He dumped the ground coffee into the basket, ran seven cups of cold water into the pot, poured it into the coffeemaker, and turned the switch to "on."

At the front of the store, Fred was simultaneously cranking on the music.

"Aha!" exclaimed Father Tim. "Vivaldi!"

His spirits were up and running.

He would glaze the wing, after all.

"Here we are. . . ."

Andrew was thumbing through a book he'd found at home. "Look at this. *Vierge et enfant,* it's called . . . the Virgin Mother's robe is black. Foreshadowing the cross, perhaps."

"No," he said. "No black." He held the angel carefully, glazing the wing with light, rapid brushstrokes. Before it dried, he'd use his little finger to insinuate the separation of the feathers.

"Now, then," said Andrew, "this is wonderful. Raphael's *Virgin of Loreto.* Look at the scarlet of her gown— something more like a rich coral, really."

"Rich coral. That sounds good."

Andrew thumbed the pages.

"Giovanni Battista Salvi's *Madonna and Child with Angels.* Again a gown of scarlet, with an overmantle of blue. Exquisite!"

"Let me see." He hiked his glasses farther up his nose. "Blue. Definitely blue. And scarlet. Yes! Mark that page, if you would."

Fred ducked through the door. "I brought th' walnut chest from th' warehouse. You want it in th' window?" he asked Andrew.

"Where the bookcase was sitting. I'll give you a hand after lunch. How did the color come up under the wax?"

"As good as it gets! It's nearly twelve, I can run out for sandwiches. . . ."

"Not for me," said Andrew. "I'm going up the hill to sample a pasta dish invented by my beautiful wife."

"And I'm off to the Grill," said Father Tim.

It was the way he stood up, he remembered afterward—the way his leg had somehow twisted, causing him to lose his balance.

As he grabbed for the sink with his left hand, he saw the angel tumble from his right; it seemed to take a very long time to fall. He heard a terrible sound escape his throat, something between a shout and a moan, as the figure crashed onto the slate floor.

Finding his balance, he looked down in horror.

The angel was shattered. He was shattered.

There was a long silence in which he and Andrew and Fred stood frozen, unmoving. He realized that his mouth was still open, forming the shout he'd heard himself make.

"Good Lord," Andrew said at last.

He wanted to burst into tears, but steeled himself. "What a bumbling fool . . ."

"Please." He felt Andrew's hand on his shoulder. "No recriminations. The head is intact, and the wing isn't so bad. What do you think, Fred? Can it be fixed?"

"I think it would take . . ."—Fred cleared his throat—"a mighty long time. Th' body's in a lot of little pieces."

Father Tim stooped and picked up

the head, and was somehow deeply moved to see the face still so serene, and so perfectly, perfectly satisfied.

Fred stepped away and returned with a box and a broom. "Let me sweep up. You go on to th' Grill."

"Yes," he said, hoarse with regret. "Yes."

"I don't reckon you'll be back today."

"Oh, yes. I will. Time is running out."

"I'll just put everything in this box," said Fred.

Andrew drew on his overcoat and muffler, looking solemn. "We can keep it and look at it again down the road. We may want to have a try at—"

"No," said Father Tim, shaking his head. "Let it go."

The adrenaline that pumped in him so furiously these last weeks had crashed with the angel. He felt confused, and suddenly old.

They sat on the sofa with a bowl of popcorn between them. A small fire crackled on the hearth.

"I finished early at the fire station and came looking for you at the Oxford . . . ," she said.

"You did?"

". . . to take you to lunch, but you'd already gone. Fred said I missed you by this much."

"How did you know where to find me?"

"Everybody knows where to find you."

"They do?"

"Yes, darling. Remember, this is a small town! Actually, I was in The Local and asked Avis if he'd seen you, and he said when he steps outside to smoke, he often sees you 'messing around' at the Oxford."

"Aha."

"Avette at the library said she'd seen you turn in there several times, and, of course, the Irish Woolen Shop, which is practically next door, said the same."

He'd never been fond of keeping a secret, at least not one of his own. Clearly, it wasn't his long suit, and he wished she would wipe that grin off her face.

She leaned her head to one side, her eyes blue and expectant. "So I don't suppose you'd like to give me a clue?"

"No deal. None. And stay away from the Oxford, you big snoop."

"But, Timothy, I wasn't snooping! We've both been so busy, I was missing you—I thought it would be fun to have lunch."

"Tell that to the judge," he said, pleased. "By the way, I wanted to drop off a note to my favorite author this morning, but your workroom door was locked." Her workroom door had never been locked before. "So . . . what are you up to?"

She took a handful of popcorn. "A

little of this and a little of that," she said, obviously pleased with herself.

"Really?"

"You know, the usual."

"Can you give me a clue?"

"No deal. None."

"None?"

She hammered down on the pop-corn. "*None!* Christmas is coming, you know."

Which, of course, explained every-thing.

He tucked the note in the pocket of her robe as she took her morning shower.

Someone had done a study with six- to eight-year-olds, asking them to de-fine love, and he'd run across the results on the Internet.

When you love somebody, your eye lashes go up and down and little stars come out of you.

When someone loves you, the way they

say your name is different. You know that your name is safe in their mouth.

Taking you to dinner Wednesday eve. Yours until heaven and then forever, T

P.S. He calls His sheep by name, and our names are safe in His mouth.

Seven

*W*hat had, in the beginning, belonged to him had come to belong to Andrew and Fred also. He felt he'd let everyone down by dropping the angel.

He was willing, however, to let go of this needless guilt and move on.

It was ironic that he'd lost two angels in recent years. Though it had been a glad sacrifice, he'd given the first to his next-door neighbor and tenant, Hélène Pringle, whose life had once been formed, quite literally, around the bronze and marble figure that now sat on her mantel.

In any case, the clock was ticking on everything, including his lists. Sitting at his desk by the window, he turned to the back of the partially blank book in

which he gathered and inscribed favorite quotes, and began to write.

Dooley, digital camera
Sammy, cable-knit sweater, L
Sissy/Sassy, backpacks

He got up and hurried along the hall
to Cynthia's workroom and knocked
on the locked door. "Kavanagh, what
about books for the girls?"
"*Little Women!*"
"Good," he said, scribbling.
"*Narnia. Nancy Drew.*"
"What about *Wind in the Willows*?"
"We gave them that last year!"
"What do you think about *Uncle Re-
mus*?" he called through the door.
"Brilliant! They'll love *Uncle Remus,*
especially if their grandpaw reads it
aloud to them."
"I thought we could stick all the
books in their backpacks! Save on
wrapping."
"Could you give Hope a call right

away? Make sure she has these on hand or can order them in time. Oh, and, dearest—add *Anne of Green Gables* in the eight-volume set."

"Consider it done!" They were certainly doing their part for Happy Endings. "What about a housecoat for Louella?"

"Perfect! Extra large, with sleeves, and a zipper in front. Leave the list on the kitchen island, and I'll take care of what you can't get to. And remember your haircut for the Christmas Eve service."

Blast. He'd rather take a whipping. . . .

"I hear Joe Ivey is cutting hair at home," she informed him.

He wasn't fond of yelling through a door. "I'll take care of it! And by the way, what's that *smell* coming from your workroom?"

"Curiosity killed the cat, Timothy!"

Back he trotted to his desk. Busy signal at Happy Endings. He hoped it was an incoming book order a half mile long.

Puny, crock pot
Nurses @ Hope House, chocolates, 4 dzn, reserve at Local
Children's Hosp., as above . . .
Andrew, my cpy early ed. Oxfd Bk Eng Verse
Fred, Garden spade, Dora's Hdwe
Jonathan Tolson and siblings, ask Cyn

He heard his good dog thump from the sofa to the floor and pad to the desk, where he gazed up with brown and solemn eyes.

"Hey, buddyroe."

And what might he give the one who had brightened his days and encouraged his spirits and forgiven his shortcomings and listened to him ramble while actually appearing interested?

He scratched behind the pair of willing ears. "When we get out to Meadowgate, you can wallow in the creek, and I won't yell; I won't even try to stop you from chasing squirrels. After all, life is short, carpe diem!"

Barnabas yawned.

"In the meantime . . ."

He opened the drawer and gave his dog one of the treats that caused his desk and everything in it to reek of smoked bacon.

When he completed the gift list, he began another for food shopping. The list for Dooley's welcome-home banquet was a no-brainer: steak and the ingredients for chocolate pie.

Aloud, he counted heads for dinner on Christmas Day.

"Dooley, Sammy, Lon Burtie, Poo, Jessie, Harley, Hélène, Louella, Scott Murphy, the two Kavanaghs . . . eleven!" Who else?

"Lord, we have room for one more!"

Oysters . . .

But how many? Chances are, his favorite thing on the menu wouldn't be
so popular with this assembly.

Two pints, he wrote.

Heavy cream
10-lb ham, bone in

. . . He would bake the ham; Cynthia
would trot out her unbeatable oyster
pie, a vast bowl of ambrosia, and a
sweet-potato casserole; Hélène would
bring the haricots verts, and Harley had
promised a pan of his famous fudge
brownies. What's more, Puny was baking a cheesecake and making cranberry
relish; Louella was contributing yeast
rolls from the Hope House kitchen;
and rumor suggested that Esther Bolick
was dropping off a two-layer orange
marmalade . . .

. . . altogether a veritable minefield
for the family diabetic, but he'd gotten
handy at negotiating minefields.

He eyed the clock with anxiety, feeling pressed to quit the list and get down to the Oxford. But, no! Absolutely not. He forced himself to lean back in the chair as if he were actually relaxed.

He was forthwith assaulted by the anxiety of moving ahead on his homily for the midnight Christmas Eve service at Lord's Chapel, then rummaging through the basement for the Christmas-tree stand and calling The Local about the chocolates and ringing Hope to make sure she had everything on the list and checking with the Woolen Shop about Sammy's sweater—

Blast it! *No!* He would not forfeit the glad rewards of this rare, unhurried moment.

He took a deep breath, exhaled, and closed his eyes.

Thank you, Lord, for the grace of an untroubled spirit, and for the blessings which are ours in numbers too great to count or even recognize. . . .

He sat for some time, giving thanks, and then, without precisely meaning to, remembering. . . .

Sometime before Christmas, he noticed that his mother's usually serene countenance was pale and drawn; she hardly seemed herself. Then came the terrible pain in her side.

"Run!" commanded his father. "Get Peggy!"

His heart pounding into his throat, he raced as fast as his legs would carry him to the small house behind the privet hedge at the end of the lane.

It was late afternoon, and cold. He found Peggy hanging the wash on a line in front of her fireplace.

"Somethin's wrong with Mama! You got to come."

Peggy had put out the fire, thrown on her old gray coat, and hand in hand, they raced along the rutted and frozen lane.

When they got to the big white house in the stand of oaks, the black Buick was gone.

"Yo' daddy done took 'er to Memphis," said Peggy, squeezing his hand, hard.

Memphis. Where the hospital was. He had held back his tears until now.

For a long time, he stood at the front door to see if his father might change his mind and bring her home and let Dr. Franklin make her well with the medicine in his black bag.

But the car didn't appear along the driveway, and, shortly after dark, Peggy took him down the lane to her house and fed him cornbread and milk and mashed sweet potato with molasses, and made him a pallet of worn quilts by the fireplace.

He would always remember the way Peggy's house smelled—like fireplace ashes and fried bacon and cold biscuits; it was a smell that made him feel safe. Nor would he ever forget how the kerosene lamp on the kitchen table made shadows flicker and dance along the walls that night, and the way Peggy prayed, aloud and urgent, raising her hands heavenward and talking to God as if He were right there in the room.

Here it was nearly Christmas, an' he thought th' good Lord had forgot, but, nossir, he'd been settin' on th' side of th' bed this mornin' when th' idea started comin.' Hit was like turnin' on a spigot an' gettin' a little squirt or two, then, first thing you knowed, hit was gushin' out.

A jewelry tray! By jing, that was th' ticket.

Her brother, Willard, had sent 'er a brooch from France when he was in th' war; she kep' it in th' dresser drawer. An' Willard had give 'er a string of pearls another time, which she kep' in a little whatnot in th' kitchen. He, hisself, had give 'er earrings one time, which she'd laid up on the mantelpiece some years back, which was where they laid to this day. A jewelry tray would collect all that. Maybe he'd put a little dab of felt on th' bottom.

Boys, was he glad t' git that notion over with!

He pulled on his old robe and shuffled up the hall to the kitchen and looked out the window to the frozen grass, then went to the counter and lifted the lid on the cold pot.

Yessir, hit was pinto bean weather, all right. He drained the soaking water off the beans and held the pot under the spigot and added fresh, then set the pot on the stove and turned on the burner. With a little dab of cornbread an' some chopped onion, boys howdy, him an' Rose would have a feast. . . .

He was countin' hisself a happy man, amen and hallelujah.

Outfitted in running gear, Father Tim made the trek to Hope House with a shopping bag over his arm and Barnabas on the red leash. In recent months, he'd been allowed to leave Barnabas at the main-floor nurses' station, instead of leashed to a post in the lobby.

"For you, my friend," he said to Ben Isaac Berman in Room Number Seven, the only domicile in Hope House with a CD player.

"Bach!" said Ben Isaac, looking with sparkling eyes at his new CD. They embraced with affection. "Thank you, Father! When are you coming for a long visit? We must have our talk about Marcus Aurelius!"

"Ah, yes," said Father Tim. "Marcus Aurelius—the department-store magnate!"

He liked to hear the handsome old man laugh.

"Here's a quote from the emperor himself," said Father Tim, "and a fine one it is: 'The first rule is to keep an untroubled spirit. The second is to look things in the face and know them for what they are.'"

Ben Isaac considered this and nodded, approving. "I must write that down."

"I'll see you the first week of January," Father Tim promised. "Book it! And if I don't see you again beforehand, Happy Hanukkah!"

"Merry Christmas, Father!" Ben Isaac called after him. "What was that first rule again?"

"Keep an untroubled spirit!"

He moved along the hall to Miss Pattie's room, where he found her sleeping. He prayed for her silently, asking God for a shower of blessings as she looked toward her ninetieth year.

Though Louella's door was open, there was no Louella.

"Louella! Are you here?"

Doris Green trundled by on her

walker, with a pack of Camels and a lighter in the basket. "She's workin' to-day."

"Working?"

"Baking biscuits. In the kitchen. Once a week. Four hours. Eight dollars an hour."

"Thank you, Doris." A fount of information!

He found Louella in the kitchen, wearing an apron and using a pint Mason jar to cut biscuits from a sheet of risen dough.

"Louella!" He was dumbfounded, to say the least.

She looked up and grinned broadly. "Hey, honey."

"What on earth are you doing?"

"Earnin' me some Christmas money."

"Well, I'll say."

"Ever'body took a fit over my biscuits a while back, so I say I'll bake once a week 'til Christmas, but lunch only an' no breakfast, an' they say,

'Here's a apron.' Last time you come, I forgot t' tell you!"

"My goodness." Would wonders never cease? "You'll need someone to take you Christmas shopping!" She could go with him when he dashed to Wesley. . . .

"No, honey, I done ordered online."

"*Online?* You're *online?*"

"Law, no, not me. Doris Green! She be hooked up all over Creation, she even talk to 'er grandson on a Navy boat in th' *ocean.*"

"Good gracious." CyberMitford!

"But this is th' last of my workin' days right here, you're lookin' at 'em. It messes with my soaps."

"Aha. Well. We're looking forward to seeing you on Christmas Day; Scott will pick you up and I'll bring you home. I left a little something in your room."

"Is it what I think it is?"

"It is!"

"Bright Cherry?"

"The very same!"

"I done gouged down in my ol' tube 'til they ain't a scrap left! I'm so pale I be lookin' like white folks."

"You look like a million bucks after taxes," he said, kissing her on the cheek.

He found himself grinning all the way down the hall.

Something was stirring in him; something strong and deep and definite. Suffice it to say he was beginning to know that Christmas was coming—not just on the calendar but in his very soul.

This morning, Cynthia's reading had explained everything:

"'The Word became flesh and lived among us, and we have seen His glory.'"

"I'm sorry," Helen said. "I know you wanted it badly, but really, Hope, you've dodged a bullet. Look how we've struggled over the years! Why you'd want to perpetuate such misery is beyond me."

"Yes, but things are beginning to change. And this is our best Christmas season ever."

The phone line crackled sharply as it often did during their daily talk after locking up Happy Endings; it was Helen's cell phone as she strolled about on her terrace overlooking the pool.

"Come to Florida, for heaven's sake, where the sun kisses your cheeks and sea breezes ruffle your hair. I always thought that little *knot* thing you do with your hair makes you look like an old maid. When you get here, we'll cut it short and highlight it—I have just the person. . . ."

"No," said Hope. "I'm not coming to Florida. It's settled—I'm going to live with Louise."

"You know what I have to say about that dead end."

She did indeed know, and could not

bear to hear it again. "Customer!" said Hope. "They're knocking on the door, I must run." She and Helen were in agreement about one thing: Customers rule.

She ran to the door and unlocked it, and felt at once a shiver of happiness. Scott was wearing his usual good-humored smile and a toboggan that made her burst into laughter.

"Are you a customer?" she asked.

"Absolutely!" He withdrew a piece of paper from his jacket pocket. "And here's my list to prove it."

"Oh, good!" she said, relieved that she hadn't deceived Helen. "I was just going up to turn on the tree lights. Want to come with me?"

"I do! Several people are out front waiting for the lights to come on—it's becoming a special Main Street attraction, I think."

"Our tree!" she said, incredulous. "A special attraction!"

He held out his hand, and she took it,

and together they walked across the creaking floor and up the stairs to the room above the shop.

Instead of heading to the monument, he walked south with Barnabas to the Oxford, where, in the glow of the streetlamp, he unlocked the door and stepped inside.

> "... *unto us a child is born,*
> *Unto us a Son is given,*
> *God himself comes down from heaven.*
> *Sing O sing, this blessed morn."*

Someone had left the CD player on. He went to the cabinet to turn it off, but chose instead the glad company of music.

Though he seldom made a visitation at night, he felt oddly at home in this dark and wax-scented room, secure somehow against the vagaries of a world where wars and rumours of wars

perpetually threatened, and hardly anything seemed dependable.

His work, however, was practically
calling his name. With Barnabas at his
heels, he quickened his step to the back
room, eager as a child to see what he
and Fred and Andrew had accom-
plished, and how far they'd come. . . .

Though what he was doing had no
deep or earth-shaking significance,
God seemed to care that he didn't blow
it; He seemed to be guiding his hands,
his instincts, his concentration.

Sometimes he and Fred would work
for an hour or more without uttering a
word, so deep was their absorption.
When he regained consciousness, as it
were, he often felt he'd been somewhere else entirely, where he felt entirely at peace.

Perhaps this was the benediction of
working with one's hands instead of
one's head. Indeed, he had hotly pursued the life of the mind nearly all his
life. His mother had ardently believed

in a healthy balance of physical, mental, and spiritual activity, but as he'd gone away to school and entered into the fray of the world, the balance had slipped, and activity of the mind and spirit had triumphed. His hands, except for gardening, cooking, and washing a dog the size of a double-wide, had engaged in little more than turning the pages of a book.

And look what he'd missed! The figures in a row on the shelf were a marvel to him. Though he was hastening to get it all finished, he would be sorry to see it all end. . . .

Thanks be to God, he'd completely released the anxiety that his artistic wife would find the work amateurish or heavy-handed. It *was* amateurish! It *was* heavy-handed! But, by heaven, it was also something else, something higher, though he couldn't say what.

He shucked off his warm jacket and gloves and picked up a brush and studied it carefully, wondering if he should choose a larger size, which would cover the surface faster.

But, no. He didn't want the Holy Family to go faster. He'd developed a special tenderness toward the last of this worshipful assembly, and wanted to give them his best effort, his deepest concentration.

Indeed, it seemed to be the wont of most people in a distracted and frantic world to blast through an experience without savoring it or, later, reflecting upon it.

For him, working on the figures had slowed him down, forced him to pay attention and to savor the work of his hands. This also reminded him daily that Christmas hadn't begun the weekend after Halloween, as the shops in Wesley and even Mitford would have one think. The time of preparation was yet under way, as the crèche was yet under way—the darkness before the light was still with the world.

His heart lifted up as he dipped his

brush into the glaze that would deepen
the hues in Joseph's robe. . . .

"Lord," he said aloud, "thank You for
being with me in this. . . ."

"Come out of there, Kavanagh! It's
ten-thirty, for Pete's sake!"

"Go stand in the kitchen so I can
open the door!"

He went to the kitchen and heard her
lock up the workroom, which contained the mysterious creation that,
sight unseen, already gave him a certain
joy.

Oddly, he couldn't wait to see her, he
was famished to see her. Her angel-tree
project was a bear, and she was han-
dling it, together with Olivia Harper,
like a trouper.

She breezed in and gave him a hug
and rubbed her warm nose against his
cold one and looked into his eyes with
frank and happy pleasure.

"Your eyelashes are going up and

down, and little stars are coming out of you," he said.

They were leaving the room when Hope saw it.

It was the smallest bit of paper sticking up between the old pine floorboards, where boxes of out-of-date schoolbooks had sat for years.

Hope knelt on one knee and removed a pin from her hair, using the pin to catch the paper and ease it upward. It was an envelope, brittle with age and bearing no postmark.

"Look!" she whispered. Scott knelt, too.

The pin slipped from her fingers and fell into the crack, along with the envelope. She took another pin from her hair, engaged the envelope once more, and pulled it from the crack.

"Good work," said Scott.

She lifted the flap and saw that it contained a letter.

"'For my little sister at Christmas,'" she read aloud from the faded inscription on the envelope.

They stood and walked into the circle of light cast by the tree, where she lifted the flap and removed the letter. The message was written on a single sheet; the once-black ink had paled to a faint reddish color, like the stain of berries.

Slowly, and with reverence, she spoke what was written in a careful hand on the yellowed paper.

Christmas, 1932
My dear little sister,

I am thinking of you this year with special feeling. I know how you enjoy having notes from me, and I must admit you are a very fine note-writer yourself.

I would like to take this opportunity to say that you are dear to me, and I am proud of you. You please me very much with your fine reading, which I can say from experience is a hard thing to grasp.

It is my fond hope that you will like your gift. Please know that it was chosen with much affection, and hope for your bright future by

Your devoted brother

"Oh," she said, moved. She held the letter as if it were something deeply personal and long desired.

"Hope."

"Yes?" She felt her hair slipping loose from its careful bun.

"It's amazing that this letter says some of the things I've been wanting to say to you."

"Really?"

He stood behind her and put his arms around her and held her close; the lights of the tree turned the empty room into a prism of color.

"I'd like to take this opportunity to say that you are dear to me, and I am proud of you."

She felt a slow warmth rising in her, a quiet and surpassing joy.

"It is my fond hope," he said, reading from the letter in her hand, "that you will like your gift. Please know that it was chosen with much affection, and hope for your bright future by your devoted friend and brother in Christ."

She held her breath, unspeaking; her hair fell to her shoulders.

"I've been wondering how to say it," he told her. "And someone said it for me, all those years ago."

He placed a small box in her hand. "Please don't open 'til Christmas," he whispered, holding her in his arms as if there were all the time in the world to stand in this room with the glittering tree, and the letter, and the sense of promise that lay ahead.

Eight

He wasn't much on checking his e-mail these days, and was flattered and mildly thrilled when he saw a queue of sixteen messages waiting.

Where to begin?

Where any priest with common sense would begin—with his bishop.

<Timothy,

<Remember the days when, emulating the proud endeavor of the good St. Paul, I wrote all important missives by hand?

<My friend, those days may be gone forever! Albeit, I'm quick to assure you that this cyber message is important.

<Heads up:

<I will almost certainly have
something for you early next year.
As you might expect, it isn't
anything fancy, and God knows, it
will be a challenge. Yet I admit I'm
patently envious.

<Can't say more at this time, but
will be in touch after the holy days,
and we shall see what's what (I do
recall, by the way, that you're
spending next year at the Owens'
farm, and this would not be a
conflict).

<Am doing as you have long
suggested, and spending more time
with my "borrowed" grandchildren.
Their several years in our lives have
added immeasurably to our health,
strength, and joy, though Martha
and I still mourn the loss of their
true grandparents and our

irreplaceable friends. I'll see to it
that you get an attachment with this
e-mail—photos of our fishing trip to
the Outer Banks. I'm glad God has
given you a pair of borrowed
grans, as well!

<As you know, The Dreaded Seven
Two arrives this summer, and I'll be
grazing in the pasture with you and
the other old goats. Heaven help
me—in dog years, I'm dead!

<I can't imagine what a retired
bishop is supposed to do with
himself. Thus far, a trip to Disney
World intrigues me most. (And, no
indeed, writing a book is not an
option.)

<As all monies have been raised
for the cathedral, and all plans
drawn and approved (an agony
beyond compare), we expect to
celebrate the groundbreaking only

days before I retire on June 15. You and C <u>must</u> be with us for that miraculous event.

<I trust you and your beautiful bride are well and happy and that Dooley is excelling in school and making you proud. May God bless you mightily at this extraordinary season, giving you a supernatural sense of His mercy, grace and peace.

<†Stuart

.　.　.

<Fr Tim,

<Dr says all looks good, I expect to be a grandma when I see you!!! Emily & Jack encouraged, as is yrs truly. All tests say it's a girl!

<Thanx for prayers, a scary time. Don't stop.

<Harold has nearly starved, I sent him a pot roast UPS overnite it cost

out the kazoo but saved his life. He
is taking time off to drive down this
week and stay through January 10
when we come home to Mitford,
and the other grandma takes over.
Please pray for Snickers, he will
have to ride in a car which always
makes him throw up.

<Have been thinking about all that
running & jogging you do, have
never been a fan of that. How
about this~

<Begin by standing behind your
house with a 5 lb potato sack in
each hand. Extend your arms
straight out to your sides and hold
them there as long as you can.

<After a few weeks, move up to 10
lb sacks and then 50 lb sacks and
finally get to where you can lift a
100 lb potato sack in each hand
and hold your arms straight out for
a full minute.

<Next . . . start putting a few potatoes in the sacks, but be careful not to overdo.

<Ha ha.

<A little present is in the mail to you & Cynthia. I found shoes to go with my new navy dress for England in May. Now I have to look for a coat because they say May can be cold at night. I think it should be navy not black, Emily says they wear black with navy only in New York. But it seems so impractical to buy a navy coat to wear with just one outfit. What do you think? Black coat or navy coat?

<Merry Christmas!

<Love, Emma

                  . . .

<Dear Father Tim,

<Everyone at St. John's sends you and Cynthia a wish for the most

blessed of Christmastides, we shall always think of you as family.

<Morris has composed a perfectly breathtaking Christmas cantata. When Sam and I heard it in rehearsal, we both wept like infants. People will be coming from across, and we are all working like Trojans to get our baking done for a little refreshment afterward.

<It has been cold here! Someone professed to have seen a flake or two of snow, but that report is not generally believed. The ponies have come back!

<I am sorry to report there are quite a few who cannot forgive Jeffrey Tolson, though Sam and I plainly see God's healing there. Sam believes all will be smoothed over with time. Your Jonathan is doing so well in school, you and Cynthia would be proud.

<Must run. Have six dozen cookies to bake! Know that much love comes your way from a little speck in the Atlantic!

<Affectionately,
<Marion

"Miss Betty, what if I was t' walk aroun' in th' yard?"

"The doctor said you can, Uncle Billy, but only when spring comes. It's too cold now."

He peered over her shoulder and into the cook pot. Collards! His all-time favorite. An' a big, fat hen a-roastin' in th' oven! Maybe he'd died in th' hospital a few months back an' went to heaven.

"If I was t' dress warm, how'd that be?"

"I don't think so, Uncle Billy. Wait 'til May when th' flowers start to bloom, that'd be a good time."

May?

A man oughtn't to have t' wait 'til May t' leave 'is house! He had important things t' do. Besides, he could be dead an' gone by May.

"What would you like best of anything?" Father Tim asked Sissy and Sassy, who flanked him on the study sofa.

"Books!" they exclaimed as one.

His order was waiting by Hope's cash register, gift-wrapped and ready to go. "What else?"

"Goldfish!" said Sissy, who looked at him with the inquisitive green eyes he loved.

"Ice skates!" said Sassy, whose infectious smile had always done him in.

Why had he asked such a question? Why couldn't he leave well enough alone, and make do with books? The answer was simple—these were his grandchildren!

"Consider it done," he said, patting a bony knee on either side.

Sassy poked his arm. "What would *you* like best of anything, Granpaw?"

"Ah. A fine question. Let me see." He dropped his head and put his hand over his eyes.

"He's thinking," said Sissy, nodding with approval.

Peace on earth, that's what he wanted.

"Healthy siblings for you two!" he said, naming another front-runner.

"What is siblings?" asked Sassy.

"A sibling is a brother or sister."

"One of each," said Sissy. "That's what I prayed for."

"So how about a trip down the street?"

"Sweet Stuff!" they chorused.

He had just delivered the girls home from Sweet Stuff and was on his way to the Oxford when the phone rang.

"Father Tim?"

"The same!"

"Lew Boyd, Father, I need somebody to talk to."

"My time is yours."

"Is there any way you could drop by the station?"

"Ah. Well . . . let's see. Sure thing! I've got to get gas, anyway. How about—thirty minutes?" Afterward, he'd pop down to the Oxford and work for a couple of hours. . . .

"I 'preciate it. I'll sweep you out good and give you a car fresh'ner—Ripe Peach, it's called. On th' house."

"Thanks, Lew. I'll pass on the Ripe Peach, but I'll see you in a half hour."

. . . and after the Oxford, he'd zoom to the Wesley mall and pick up a couple of goldfish and a pair of skates. Make that two pair. Then home again with the stuff to bake the chocolate pie for tomorrow—it was better if it sat overnight—and back to the Oxford for a final hour before making dinner with his good wife.

He was fairly giddy with all that had to be done, not to mention the blasted haircut he was forced to get somewhere, somehow. . . .

He had no intention of answering the phone when it rang again, but his hand shot forth like an arrow, and there he stood, saying, "Hello!"

"Father Tim?"

"Is that you, Esther?"

"It is. Father Talbot's a busy man, you know."

"Ah, yes. Packing for Australia as we speak, is my guess."

"So could you give me some advice?"

"If I can. Be glad to." He checked his watch.

"I'm only human."

"True enough."

"I hate to admit this."

"You can admit it to me."

"You know Ol' Man Mueller?"

"Oh, yes."

"Every Christmas, I take him an orange marmalade."

"That's *very* good of you, Esther."

"Scripture tells us to visit the poor. But I don't want to do it anymore."

"Aha."

"I was crossin' Main Street the other day, an' the old goat nearly ran over me—he didn't even slow down."

"Don't take it personally, Esther."

"After Gene and I have slogged out to his place every Christmas Eve in th' pitch-black dark to deliver his cake!"

"I think his eyesight is going, he nearly bagged me a couple of times."

"Would I be a hypocrite if I didn't want to take 'im a cake but did it anyway? Or would I be worse if I just thought about doin' it an' didn't do it all?"

"In my humble opinion? Worse!"

He heard her sigh. "I knew you'd say that."

Uncle Billy was zipping his jacket when his wife walked into the kitchen wearing a pink chenille bathrobe and a small black cocktail hat with a mashed veil.

"Where do you think you're going, Bill Watson?"

"Down th' street!" he hollered, grabbing his cane from the back of the chair.

"You sit down over yonder and be sick! If you get well, they won't send Miss Betty to cook for us, and that'll be a fine kettle of fish." The mashed veil trembled.

"They ain't no pot of collards worth bein' tied up like a chain-gang prisoner." He pulled an old wool hat down over his ears and searched his pockets for gloves. "I got t' see about some *lumber!"*

"*Mumbler?* I can hear every word I say, plain as day. It's you who's the mumbler, Bill Watson! Where are you going down the street?"

"I'm goin' t' see Santy!" he yelled at the top of his lungs.

"Santy!" exclaimed his wife.

Right there it was—all the proof a man needed that she could hear anything she dadblame wanted t' hear.

"You tell him not to come down the chimney this year," she said. "It's full of squirrels. Tell him to come in the back door, we'll leave the screen unlatched."

His wife's face had lit up like a young 'un's. As he went down the steps, one at a time, he felt mighty glad t' have th' Lord in on what he was about to do.

It wasn't the first time he'd counseled in a pickup truck with the heater blasting.

"I been fixin' t' talk t' you for a good while," said Lew. "But since me an' Earlene run off to a JP an' didn't let you marry us, it didn't seem right t' bother you."

"It's no bother at all, Lew. What's on your mind?"

Lew checked his Timex. "I got t' talk fast, we got a Honda comin' in for brake shoes."

"Aha."

"Thing is, I married Earlene even if she is takin' care of her mama 'til she passes, an' even if she does want t' stay at th' flour comp'ny 'til she collects 'er retirement."

"I see."

"But I miss 'er. I feel lonesome as a buck, you know what I mean?"

"I know precisely what you mean."

"But th' deal's done—she lives with 'er mama an' can't even tell 'er she's married. Earlene's sisters say it would kill 'er straight off, she's way up in 'er nineties an' has a real bad heart. So on top of it all, we're keepin' it a secret. I ain't told nobody but you, 'cause if I did, th' news would run up th' road quick as a scalded dog."

"That's true."

"An', see, I feel like it ain't right of me to expect anything but what we agreed on before we was married."

"Were you willing to wait then?"

"I was then, but mostly I ain't now."

"Did you marry her because you love her or because you were a lonely widower?"

"I ain't goin' t' lie. It was some of both. But mostly because I love 'er. She's a fine woman, an' that's a fact."

"Have you talked to God about this?"

"I go t' church now an' again, but I ain't whole hog on religion."

"Why is that?"

Lew shrugged. "Seem like he wouldn't want t' mess with me."

"Why wouldn't He?"

"I don't know. I've done a good bit of wrong in my life."

"So have I."

"Not you!"

"Yes, me."

"I'll be dogged."

"I'm a sinner saved by grace, Lew, not by works. It doesn't matter a whit that I'm a priest. What matters is that we surrender our hearts to God and receive His forgiveness, and come into personal relationship with His Son."

"Earlene, she's got that kind of thing with, you know . . ." He pointed up.

"Would you like to have it?"

Lew gazed out the driver's window, then turned and looked at Father Tim. Tears streamed down his roughly shaven face. "I don't know, I guess I ain't ready t' do nothin' like that."

"When you are, there's a simple prayer that will usher you into His presence and change your life for all time—if you pray it with a true heart."

Lew wiped his eyes on his jacket sleeve.

"How simple is it?"

"This simple: Dear God, thank You for loving me and for sending Your Son to die for my sins. I sincerely repent of my sins and receive Christ as my personal Savior. Now, as Your child, I turn my entire life over to You."

"That's it?"

"That's it."

"I don't know about turnin' my entire life over."

"An entire life is a pretty hard thing to manage alone."

"Yessir."

There was a thoughtful silence as the heater blasted full throttle.

"Meanwhile," said Father Tim, "why don't we pray about what you've just told me?"

"Yessir. I 'preciate it." Lew bowed his head.

"Lord, thank You for Your mercy and grace. You know the circumstances, and You've heard Lew's heart on this hard thing.

"All we ask, Father, is that Your will be done.

"In the mighty name of Jesus, Your Son and our Savior, amen."

"Beggin' your pardon, Father, but that don't seem like much t' ask."

"It's the prayer that never fails, Lew."

"Never fails?"

"Never. I hope you'll pray it in the days and weeks to come."

Lew considered this. "Exactly what was it again?"

"Thy will be done."

Lew nodded, thoughtful. "OK. All right. I can do that. I don't see as there's anything to lose."

"Good thinking, my friend!"

"Here comes m' Honda. *Whoa!* He don't have no brakes left a'tall, looks like."

Father Tim opened the passenger door and stepped down. "Nice truck," he said, giving the right front tire an amiable kick.

> *Dear Emma,*
> *Praying faithfully.*
> *Black coat.*
> *Yours truly,*
> *Fr Tim*

Andrew surveyed the work to date, standing before the laden shelf with his arms crossed.

"Father, you seem to have stumbled on a latent talent here."

"Surely not!" He felt the sudden dart of happiness in hearing such a thing.

"The way you've put the colors together . . ."

"I've had a lot of help, as you recall."

"Well, yes, but you had to do the mixing and applying. This old shepherd is particularly appealing, I think, with his simple brown robe. Well done!"

"Thank you. I confess I loved that figure, with its bowed head and earnest countenance." He didn't know when he'd been so thankful for a bit of praise.

"You've always struck me as someone who might write poetry—have a drawerful of it somewhere." Andrew turned and smiled. "Would I be right?"

Father Tim laughed. "George Herbert wrote all my poetry for me."

"Or an essayist, perhaps. Ever tried the essay?"

"Tried and failed!"

"Ah, well. A man has his limits. I must tell you I've liked having this crowd around the place, they've added a certain grace. I'll miss the lot of you when Christmas comes. By the way, any more thoughts about a stable?"

"Not this year." Father Tim surveyed the work remaining to be done. "A man has his limits," he said, grinning.

He'd been so busy, the bald truth had hardly sunk in. But in just a few days, one of the most important institutions in Mitford would vanish in the mists of history.

As far as some people were concerned, losing the Grill was akin to losing an arm or a leg, or at least a couple of digits. No one, however, had been game to keep the Grill up and running, even if Edith Mallory had gone for it, as the limited seating didn't make for much of a bottom line.

Indeed, the historic cooking and refrigeration apparatus was scheduled to be ripped out soon after closing and, according to rumor, hauled to the dump with hardly a fare-thee-well. Then, in would march the shoe store, nailing its shelves to the walls. . . .

He was just setting out his brushes when Mule popped his head in the door.

"Got a minute?"

Father Tim made a move to sprint to the door and distract his visitor, but it was too late. Mule trotted in, gaping at the figures lining the shelf.

"Man! What're y'all doin' in here? Look at this!"

"This is undercover stuff, never to be mentioned." Andrew must have stepped out to the bank. . . .

"Ain't that a sight," Mule said, reverent. "That's th' shepherds an' wise men an' all!"

"Right. And don't say a word about it to anybody!" His pulpit voice, he hoped, would underline this command.

"You're doin' all this?"

"With a little help from my friends."

"How come you didn't get me in on th' deal? I'm your friend."

"True."

"Who's this?"

"Joseph."

Mule's eyes were wide. "An' look at th' sheep, an' that donkey. I always liked a donkey. This is a sight for sore eyes; you need t' set this up in a display window someplace. Course, your camel don't look so hot."

"He hasn't been painted yet."

"You ought t' give me a shot at it; I did our bathroom and front porch."

"Dooley gets to paint the camel. He'll be home tomorrow night." Tomorrow night!

"Where's th' Baby Jesus at?"

Father Tim took the manger and child from the box, and cradled the piece in his hands.

Mule cleared his throat. "Well," he said. "Ain't that somethin'? So where's th' stable in this deal?"

"Don't have a stable."

"You got to have a stable."

"I don't have time to build a stable—maybe next year."

"I've built a thing or two in my time. You could get an orange crate from Avis, break that sucker down, hammer in a few nails, an' you'd have a stable."

"I'll catch you for lunch tomorrow."

"I been thinkin.' Somebody ought t' do somethin' for Percy an' Velma, you know what I'm sayin'? Seems like somethin' ought to *happen* on their last day."

"I thought Coot Hendrik was cooking up a celebration."

"Never got it organized, plus he's down with walkin' pneumonia."

"Ah." He took a deep breath.

"There's not much time, but . . . why don't we give them a party?"

Mule smoked this over. "You mean you an' me?"

"Somebody needs to get things rolling."

"Where at?"

"At the Grill. Christmas Eve. Right after lunch when they close."

"Who'll do th' food? It don't seem right to ask Percy—"

"If it's after lunch, nobody needs food. Or maybe we could just have, I don't know, *dessert.*"

"What kind of dessert?"

"Beats me, we just got this idea. Maybe a couple of cakes. And I'll make the coffee. I know how to operate the coffee machine, he's had it for a hundred years."

Mule looked suspicious. "So who'll pick up th' tab for th' cakes?"

"We'll pass the hat. Maybe collect enough to get Percy and Velma a ticket

to Washington, to see the cherry blossoms. What do you think?"

"Yeah!" said Mule, grinning. "Great
idea!"

"So see you for lunch tomorrow!"
Father Tim felt his adrenaline pump up
a notch.

What was he thinking, to add a party
at the Grill on the same day of the
Christmas Eve mass at Lord's Chapel,
and the trimming of the tree, and the
secret setup of the Nativity scene in the
living room, and getting everything in
order for their big dinner on Christmas
Day?

Was he out of his *mind?*

The answer, of course, was yes.

He was glazing Joseph's overgarment
when J. C. Hogan barreled into the
room.

"Whoa!" said Father Tim. What was
this, anyway, Grand Central Station?

J.C. slung his bulging, unzipped briefcase into a chair. "I hear you're livin' down here now, got a cot in th' back room."

"Who let you in?"

"I let myself in. Fred's unloadin' a truck in the alley, an' Andrew's up th' street." He unfurled a pocket handkerchief and wiped his face. "What's goin' on? I been lookin' for your obit."

"Who told you I'm down here?"

"Everybody knows you're down here. So what's that?"

"What's what?"

"What's that you're paintin'? Looks like some of my kin people." J.C. cackled.

"Look, J.C., you need to keep this to yourself. The whole thing is meant to be a surprise for Cynthia. I'd like your word."

"I'm not much on keepin' secrets!" J.C. eyed the figures on the shelf. "Don't tell me you did all this!"

"I didn't do all this."

"Looks like a Nativity scene. . . ."

"It is. And, believe me—if you say anything to anybody, I'll personally knock you in the head."

"OK, all right, they'll never hear it from me. Man, this is great. I didn't know you could do stuff like this."

"Neither did I."

"Where's your stable?"

"Don't have a stable."

"Everybody knows you got to have a *stable* for a *Nativity* scene. A little baby can't just lay out in th' *weather*, you know what I'm sayin'?"

"Preacher?" Uncle Billy stuck his head in the door.

"Uncle Billy! What are you doing downtown?"

"Buyin' lumber!" said the old man, his gold tooth gleaming. "Dora, she tol' me you're workin' here."

"Did Hoppy say you could be out and about?"

"He said I could walk aroun' in th' yard. I figured a man could exchange that f'r walkin' down th' street."

"What kind of lumber?"

He tapped the bundle under his arm. "I'm makin' Rose a present. Christmas is comin,' don't you know."

"Look," said the *Muse* editor, "I'm outta here. Let's have lunch at th' tea shop after Christmas."

"Will do. By the way, we're getting together a little celebration for Percy and Velma, right after lunch on Christmas Eve. Hope you'll be there."

"Of course I'll be there, I'm in th' dadgum newspaper business, it's my job to be there."

"Their forty-plus years at the Grill are worth a front page," said Father Tim, meaning it.

"Don't preach me a sermon, buddy-roe!" J.C. grabbed his briefcase and shot through the door,

Father Tim grinned. "Uncle Billy, no

rest for the wicked and the righteous don't need none."

Uncle Billy grinned back; he liked it when th' preacher stole one of his sayin's.

"I hope you and Miss Rose can be there. You've both got a long history with the Grill."

"Nossir, I can't make it, I've got a awful job of work t' do an' no time t' th'ow away. What's this you're a-workin' on?"

"I'm restoring a Nativity scene as a surprise for Cynthia."

The old man stared at the shelf, his mouth open. "I'll be et f'r a tater."

Father Tim realized that he liked sharing the figures; they took on added meaning when he saw them through other eyes.

"Did you *make* all them animals an' such?"

"No, sir, I only painted them. And fixed them up a little, here and there."

"They're beauteous," said Uncle Billy, deeply moved. He'd learned that word as a boy and didn't get a chance to use it much. "Beauteous!"

"Thank you."

"There's y'r wise men. An' y'r sheep. Law, they's a whole flock of 'em, an real as life! An' y'r angel—look at that! Jis' one angel, is it?"

"Yes, sir. There were two, but I dropped one and broke it." The thought pained him, still.

"An' y'r Baby Jesus, He's th' main show. Where's He at?"

Father Tim took the Babe in the manger from the box and held it forth in his hands. He felt oddly parental.

"Husky little feller!"

"He is!"

"Where's y'r stable at?"

"We don't have a stable. We've got all we can do to get the figures done by Christmas Eve."

"This crowd needs theirself a stable,"

said Uncle Billy. "Wouldn't take no time a'tall t' knock one together."

"That's easy for you to say, Uncle Billy, but I'm not much with a hammer and nails. I don't suppose you'd have a joke—a fellow needs a laugh or two to help his work along."

"I had a pretty good 'un a while back, but I've done forgot it."

"Aha!"

"M' noggin's s' full of this an' that, I cain't hardly recall m' Christian name."

"That can happen this time of year."

"Here's one t' hold you 'til I can git back t' m' joke job. A man fell in th' lake, don't you know, and was a-drownin' when a feller come along an' pulled 'im out. Th' man's preacher said, 'You ought t' give that feller fifty dollars f'r savin' y'r life!' Man said, 'Could I make that twenty-five? I was half dead when he pulled me out.'"

"Father Tim?"

"Hope! Come in, come in!" The floodgates had opened.

"Uncle Billy!" she said, extending her hand. "How are you feeling? I'm glad to see you out!"

"I'm goin' t' make it!"

Hope looked flushed, thought Father Tim. The winter cold had rouged everyone's cheeks.

"Father, I wanted to tell you something . . ."

He thought his favorite bookseller looked shy as a dove, and especially pretty into the bargain.

"It's something special, but I can come back. . . ."

Fred poked his head in the doorway and eyed the crowd. "Sorry about that, sir, I was helpin' unload a truck."

"Don't worry about it, Fred."

"There's a call for you. You want to take it out here?"

"I'm a-goin'," said Uncle Billy. "We'll see y'uns in th' funny papers."

"Thanks for the joke." said Father

Tim. "I'm going to laugh when I get a minute!"

Fred shucked off his heavy gloves. "Uncle Billy, you need a ride home?"

"Nossir, I'm rustin' like a gate hinge, I need t' trot home by m'self."

Father Tim stepped into the shop area and took the cordless from Fred.

"Tim Kavanagh here. . . .

"Yes. Yes, I do," he said. "For many years. . . .

"Strong character, immeasurably hardworking, honest and forthright in every regard. . . .

"In truth, I can't say enough good things. . . .

"Aha! Thanks be to God! I hope you'll attend to it immediately, time is certainly flying. . . ."

He paced around a Regency chest-on-chest, the phone to his ear.

"Yes, indeed, it will be good for all concerned—you have my word on it. . . .

"Well done, then. God bless you!"

He trotted to the back room, where Hope was gazing at the figures on the shelf.

She turned and smiled at him with genuine fondness. "My goodness, Father, you look like the Cheshire cat!"

"As it turns out, my dear, I have something special to tell you, too! But why don't you go first?"

She took a deep breath.

In all the years he'd known Hope Winchester, he had never seen her look so . . . *joyful,* that was it!

"I wanted to tell you . . ."

"Yes?"

". . . that I'm in love."

Tears sprang at once to his eyes.

"It's Scott, Father."

"Yes," he said. "And I have no words to express my happiness for you both."

He took out his handkerchief and wiped his eyes and gave her an enthusiastic hug.

The Good Lord had certainly picked

a fine way to fill the empty chair at their Christmas dinner table.

"Oh, and Father . . ." She opened her purse and withdrew an envelope. "Before I forget, I have something to show you. . . ."

The goldfish were swimming about in a crystal bowl, hidden from view in the laundry room; the ice skates were done up in bright paper and tucked away on the floor of his closet; the refrigerator and pantry were loaded with supplies; and he wasn't making another trip to Wesley 'til after the thaw—period, zip, end of discussion.

He'd made his list and checked it twice, and was, in a manner of speaking, wrapping things up. The issue of the haircut, however, remained unresolved.

Full of expectation, he trooped up Lilac Road to visit Joe Ivey.

"I only barber when I want to," said Joe, occupied with a cross-stitch image of Santa Claus disappearing down a chimney.

"Well, then. Do you want to?"

"Nossir," said Joe, "I don't want to."

So, one, he had given it his best shot, and failed.

And, two, there was no way on God's green earth he was putting his head in the hands of Fancy Skinner. No more lamb-to-the-slaughter for this country parson!

Three, there had been no time to do it while in Wesley today, and if he wasn't running over there again any-time soon, one of their overpriced haircuts wasn't an option, anyway.

"Fred," he said, "have you ever cut hair?"

"I cut my wife's hair once."

Once. Didn't sound encouraging.

"Turned out she looked s' much like 'er brother, they thought he'd gone t' wearin' a skirt."

"Umm."

"I was in th' doghouse for a good while. But you take my gran'daddy, he was a barber an' a half. Used to barber th' men at shearin' time. Barbered th' neighbors, too, had a good little business set up on th' back porch."

"I see."

"Ever' now an' again, he pulled teeth on th' side."

"Enterprising!" And Dooley wasn't an option, either. Dooley Barlowe had once given him what appeared to be a scallop design along his neck. He checked his watch; he had strict orders to be home in forty-five minutes. . . .

"Is it you that's wantin' a haircut?"

"It is, Fred, it is." He heaved a sigh.

"I wouldn't have said anything . . ." Fred left his sentence unfinished, but raised one eyebrow.

Time was flying; it was fish or cut bait. "What do you need to do the job?"

"Scissors an' a comb."

"I've got a comb," said Father Tim.

"I've got scissors," said Fred.

"While you're at it, I've been having a little trouble with my left molar."

They laughed. If worse came to worst, he could wear a hat when he left the house, and, as for the Christmas Eve service, it would be pretty dark in the candlelit nave, anyhow.

"Hop on your stool," said Fred, "an' I'll be right back."

He did as he was told. *Lord,* he prayed, *I'd appreciate it if You'd be in on this. . . .*

He had mentioned it to Cynthia this morning, but only in a casual, offhand way. He didn't want to get excited, it was too soon.

I will almost certainly have something for you next year. . . .

It isn't anything fancy, and God knows, it will be a challenge. . . .

But he couldn't help getting excited.

Every time he thought about it, he felt his heart beat a jot faster; he picked up his gait as he walked home, and recalled that he'd twice found himself whistling in the mall.

Nine

"*I*'ve been thinking."

"Will wonders never cease!" How he loved this earnest boy with his intense gaze and tousled hair and faithful remnant of freckles.

"I don't want my father's name anymore." Dooley stared into the blazing fire on the study hearth, his brow furrowed.

There was a long silence; the fire crackled; the clock ticked.

Dooley turned to face him. "So what if I take your name?"

Dooley Kavanagh! It was something he'd discussed with Cynthia, and prayed about more than a few times. Now he did his own staring into the fire, searching his own heart. *Lord, I need wisdom here. . . .*

Dooley's voice was hoarse with feeling. "Barlowe is a bad name to have."

"But you'll make it a good name to have."

"What do you mean?"

"Dr. Barlowe. In fact, you're already making it a good name to have. I'm proud of you, son."

"But I don't want anything of his. Nothing!"

"You have something quite precious of his—your brothers and little sister."

Though the winter dark had come, no lamps were lit; firelight illumined the study.

"If you were to take the Kavanagh name, you would do it great honor. In truth, nothing would make me prouder. Yet Barlowe is a name that came to you by a long and winding stream—I remember reading about a Barlowe who was co-captain with Sir Walter Raleigh on Raleigh's first voyage to Virginia in the sixteenth century. The fact that he helped get the ship

there and back to England was no mean
feat in those days."

Dooley shrugged.

"Your family roots are Anglo-Saxon
and can be traced to the ancient territo-
ries of England. Thus, your name em-
bodies far more than the connection
to a man who abandoned you and
brought great suffering—you might say
it's part of what you're made of . . ."

The ticking of the clock, the snoring
of his dog . . .

". . . and, son . . ."

"Yes?"

"You're made of very fine stuff."

Dooley gazed into the fire, unspeaking.

"Why don't you think about it a
while longer? Make sure of your feelings."

Dooley waited, then nodded, his lips
tight. "OK."

"Please know that I respect your feelings. Though I never thought of
changing my name, there were times

when I'd have given anything to sever connections with my own father."

Dooley looked surprised.

"We'll talk about it one of these days." He checked his watch. "You said you need to be out of here by six-thirty. It's six twenty-five."

Dooley sat back in the chair, making no move to leave. "It's going to be really good at Meadowgate next summer."

"Yes! It will be."

"I always kind of missed you and Cynthia when I was out there."

"You did?" He remembered how bereft he'd felt when Dooley chose Meadowgate over staying with them for the summer; it had wrenched his soul.

Dooley looked at his loafers.

"Anything else on your mind, son?"

"Yes, sir." Dooley took a deep breath. "I want to thank you."

"For what?"

"For everything."

What could he say? "I thank you back."

"Well . . . ," said Dooley.

"Going to a movie?"

"Out to dinner."

"Aha." That explained the blazer.

"With Lace."

He was the nosiest man on the planet, but he was keeping his mouth shut.

"It's her birthday."

"Her birthday! How old?"

"Nineteen. A year younger than me."

"*Aha*." He reached into his pocket, withdrew his wallet, and pulled out two twenties.

"Where are you taking her?"

"To Miss Sadie's."

Several people in town referred to the Gregorys' Italian restaurant, Lucera, as Miss Sadie's, given its location on the main floor of Fernbank.

"Well, then!" he said, withdrawing another twenty. Lucera was no drive-through; as he recalled, the veal piccata was a cool $24.95. "The car keys are on the hall table."

"Thanks, Dad." Dooley grinned and, making certain Mr. Jackson faced the same way on all three bills, folded them and stuck them in the pocket of his khakis. "Her curfew is eleven-thirty. I'll be in right after."

"Dooley . . ."

"Yes, sir?"

I love you, he wanted to say. "Have fun! Give Lace our love. Tell her happy birthday!"

"Yep. I will."

"Be careful."

"Yes, sir."

"Remember the heater takes a while to warm up, and the radio only gets one station."

"Got it. Catch you later."

"They're calling for snow tonight!"

Dooley disappeared through the kitchen doorway; Father Tim raced behind him into the hall.

"Dooley?"

Dooley turned; the light of the lamp by the stair shone on his face. "Yes, sir?"

"I love you," he said, hoarse as a frog.

"Where the dickens are my handle pulls?"

His wife confronted him before he'd hardly gotten up the back steps from the garbage can.

"What handle pulls is that?"

"The ones that were on my cabinets below the silver drawer! How is a body supposed to open the doors?"

"Poke a dadjing knife blade under th' door and hit'll pop right open." It was freezing cold this morning; Uncle Billy stuck one hand in his jacket pocket and brandished his cane with the other. "Let me in th' house, by johnny!"

"I'll let you in the house, Bill Watson, when you tell me what you've done with my handle pulls!"

"I give 'em t' ol' Santy, is what I done!"

"Santy, my foot!"

"He come an' wanted 'em, an I let let 'im have 'em! They ain't nothin' in them cab'nets no way, but a mess of paper cups you toted home from church."

"And *Fig Newtons,*" she said, looking thoroughly disgusted.

Dear Louise,

Thanks for calling me last night. I miss you, too. I know the house feels lonely without Mama in it, and I don't blame you for wanting to make a change, even though change can be hard. I'm learning that God wants the best for us, and if we pray for His will in our lives, He will show us how and when to move ahead, and He will help us through.

You know that I had finally given up, and then the call came to Father Tim. They phoned me at almost the final hour! How

*amazing that my letter had been lost, and
when they read it to Mrs. Mallory she
blinked her eyes yes! God was in this all
along, as He will be in helping you make a
big change in your life.*

*And that's why I'm writing. I believe
God has given me another great idea. I
hope you will think it's a great idea, too.*

*I know it sounds unbelievable, but I al-
ways loved that we shared a room, and even
our clothes. The only thing that was
absolutely, positively mine was the blue
sweater with embroidery, and I know you
sneaked and wore it when I wasn't around!*

*Louise, will you share a room with me
again?*

*Will you come to Mitford and live with
me above Happy Endings and help me
make the bookstore grow? I can't pay you
much at the beginning, but we could rent
Mama's house, which would make things
better, and as business increases and the
debt is settled, I will pay you whatever we
agree is fair.*

You have never liked your computer job at the hospital, and I think you would love the bookstore as I do. You would be so wonderful with our summer reading program. Helen never wanted to do it at all, and I'm determined we shall have one next year! You would also be the best imaginable help with the rare-books business, which is all done on the Internet.

But I have saved the best for last, which is~

<u>*I think you will love living in Mitford!*</u> *I walk almost everywhere, and know everyone in town and they know me. The people are truly wonderful (for the most part!), and I can practically promise that you'll find a new and wonderful life in Mitford, just as I have.*

Though you don't like to drive beyond Granville, it's only a hundred and nine miles to Mitford, and there are basically only <u>*three turns*</u>*—all to the left!*

I know this comes out of the blue, but if you think about it, that's where a lot of good things come from.

Love,
Hope

P.S. I decided to write this instead of calling, as it will give you a better chance to think things through. I am praying for you, and so excited that you might say yes!
P.P.S. Wish you could see the Christmas tree in the upstairs window of HE.

Hope folded the letter and put it in an ivory envelope and licked the flap and sealed it. She would tell Louise about Scott after Christmas. Her feelings toward Scott were very tender and private, she couldn't yet talk about this to anyone, though Father Tim, of course, knew.

She went to the hot plate and turned on the teakettle, then gazed around her new room with the pictures on the walls, and the bookcases full of books she had loved for years, and the lace curtains through which the Sunday-afternoon light fell upon the faded rug. She knew that she had never felt so happy, so expectant, nor so deeply grateful.

She brewed the tea and took the pot and a mug to her desk, where she thumped into her favorite old chair from her mother's screened-in porch and withdrew another sheet of ivory paper from the box. She poised her pen above it, smiling.

Scott Lewis Murphy, she wrote.

Scott Lewis Murphy

Scott Lewis Murphy

There was another name she also wished to write, but, no, she mustn't even think such a thing. She mustn't yet hope for something so precious. . . .

She poured a cup of tea and sipped it, and watched the light play upon the rug. She realized that, more than any-thing, she wanted to write the other name, but feared that doing it might bring bad luck.

Then she remembered—she didn't believe in luck anymore, good or bad. She believed in grace, and grace alone.

Mrs. Scott Lewis Murphy
Mrs. S. L. Murphy
Hope Elizabeth Murphy

Dooley cackled when he saw it.

"No way can I do that camel!"

"If I can do it, you can do it."

"No, sir, that's way too hard, I could never do it. This guy is huge."

"Yes. Agreed. But it has to be done, and I was counting on you. I've got just enough time to repaint the Virgin Mother and the Babe."

"I'm sorry. Really. But I can't. This is . . ." Dooley searched for a word, but couldn't find it. "I can't."

"You could pick a color, I could mix it, and you could brush it on. . . . We might stipple it a little. . . ."

"Just a little," said Fred.

"Nope. I can't. Really. I thought maybe it was just slap some paint on something, have some fun."

"It is fun. I promise."

"What about his ear? Would I have to do something about his ear?"

"I could do the ear."

Dooley thought for a moment. "No, sir," he said, sounding firm. "I can't do it. But everything looks great. It blows me away that you did this."

Father Tim looked at Fred, imploring.

"My wife has her quiltin' club tonight. I can give you a hand."

"Can we do it?"

"It'll take a couple of evenin's, but we can do it!"

He leaned over and gave Fred a high five.

"That's some bad paint on that camel," said Dooley. "Why would they outline his eyes with red? He looks like he's been through a couple of exam weeks, back to back. And that blanket between his humps is a really a weird color."

"So, big guy, what color would you paint the blanket?"

"Red."

"Color of your head," said Father Tim.

Dooley laughed.

"You're a poet an' don't know it!" Fred told Father Tim.

As calm as he'd meant to be, as poised as he'd planned to be, he was seeing his good intentions dashed—he was a basket case. Christmas Eve had arrived, and there was no rest for the wicked.

Paint, paint, and more paint—he had labored over that camel to beat the band, and so had Fred, and still it was a camel he wouldn't personally want to ride across the desert.

And did he have everything he needed to glaze the ham, or had he only imagined seeing a jar of molasses on the pantry shelf?

"Lord," he whispered into the dark room, "would You please handle everything that comes today? And, as Mr. Shakespeare said, 'thanks, and thanks, and ever thanks'!"

Awake at four to the sound of the wind, and up at five, he was a motor set on high speed, with no "off" switch.

"Our Father who art in heaven," he prayed aloud as he ground the coffee. The words always soothed him, even when he couldn't concentrate; they helped pull his sundered parts together. Not every prayer could be uttered in the coddling sanctuary of holy quietude; a man had to do what he had to do.

"Hallowed be thy name. . . ."

He would drive to Lord's Chapel at five o'clock, to check on the greening of the church and matters in general, then pop over to the Oxford and load

the figures into his car trunk. He'd
bring them into the house after Cynthia went upstairs to dress for the midnight service, and put them all in their
places at the foot of the tree—the
thought excited him beyond descrip-
tion. He'd escort Cynthia to the car
through the back door, and only after
coming home from Lord's Chapel
would they go into the living
room. . . .

While stuffing the filter into the basket, he remembered he'd begun the
prayer, but had no idea at what point it
had flown his mind.

"Our Father who art in heaven . . ."

He poked the buttons on the cof-
feepot until the red light came on, and
noticed the timer was blinking. He patted the pocket of his oldest robe, seek-
ing his glasses, but found only a
wadded-up Kleenex from his earlier
bout with the flu.

And the tree . . . thank God for
Harley Welch, who would go to Ashe

County for a Fraser fir and bring it over after lunch, then put it up, fill the stand with water, and carry off any unsightly limbs he'd pruned. . . .

"Hallowed be thy name!"

Off with his tattered robe and on with a pair of sweatpants over his pajama bottoms, an act that precipitated the loss of a bedroom shoe, which shucked from his foot and lodged somewhere around his knee; he shook his leg, but it wouldn't fall down through the leg of the sweatpants, so he dove in through the waistband with his right hand and hauled it out and tossed it across the room. Barnabas followed its airborne passage with his eyes, without moving his head.

As for the camel, he supposed he'd be forced to tuck it in the background, perhaps on the other side of a low-hanging branch of the tree, which they would decorate before the church service.

Aha! There was the sweater he was looking for, in the bin under the coat-rack. He pulled it on over his pajama top and layered it with a pea coat found at the Army/Navy store in Wesley.

"Thy kingdom come . . ."

He hoped Mule would remember to pick up the cakes, and that he wouldn't be slinging them around in the trunk of his Bronco without stabilizing them in some way. . . . Ah, yes, and he must remember to bring his black hat to collect the money for the tickets to Washington. He took the hat off the rack and scooted it along the polished hall floor like a bowling ball toward the pins. It rested at the foot of the staircase, where he couldn't avoid seeing it as he exited the front door on his way to the Grill at noon.

He found he was huffing like a coal-fired engine.

After returning from the monument, he must not fail to read the Morning

Office and pray. Indeed, he must concentrate his pathetic mind in prayer ASAP or be a goner the livelong day.

He grabbed his wool socks from the bin and, with one bedroom shoe on and the other off, hied to the study and thumped into his chair and pulled a wool sock onto one foot and then the other, and crammed his feet into his lug-sole boots and tied the laces.

To the kitchen door, then, snatching his cap and the red leash from the rack as he went, and out the door he flew, closing it behind him.

"The first rule is to keep an untroubled spirit," he exclaimed, his breath vaporizing on the frosty air. "The second is to look things in the face and know them for what they are!"

He was looking things in the face and knowing them for what they are. "And they are . . . ," he huffed, fishing for a word, *"berserk!"*

It was blowing out here, yes indeed, and the thermometer reading sat square on the nose of twenty degrees. He retrieved his gloves from one pocket and unraveled a wool scarf from the other.

"Our Father . . ." He wound the scarf about his neck and shook his head as if to clear it; his brain was chopped liver.

". . . who art in Heaven." He pulled his hat down over his ears before it ended up on a lamppost in Johnson City.

Sighing deeply, which filled his lungs with a blast of frigid air, he looked at the red leash dangling from his gloved hand and heard his dog barking in the kitchen.

"*Surpri-i-ise!*"

"Here we come, ready or not!"

A Mitford crowd always arrived early, and today was no exception.

"Merry Christmas!"

"Surprise! Surprise!"

"We ain't hardly got th' dishes

washed," said Percy, drying his hands on his apron.

"Take that apron *off,* it's party time!" Lois Holshouser, who was retired from teaching drama at Wesley High and wanted more fun in her life, untied Percy's apron and flung it over the counter, where it landed on a cake box.

"Watch it!" said Mule. He'd hauled those cakes around all morning, slowing down for every bump in the road.

"We've got to get these cakes out of the box!" said Father Tim. Did Mule think cakes jumped out of the box and served themselves? "Here," he said, setting a stack of plates on the counter.

"What d'you want me to do with these?"

"Start cutting cake, and cut it thin— it's got to feed the Roman legions."

"What do I cut with?"

"A *knife!*" He slid one along the counter.

"Man!" said Mule. "You should of bought this place an' gone t' runnin' it.'"

"Plastic forks, plastic forks," said Father Tim, searching under the counter. "Percy! Where are the plastic forks?"

"Down under th' bread box!" said Percy. People were crawling around in his place like worms in a can; it was all he could do to keep from hollering, "Set *down*, for Pete's sake!"

"Hey, Mule, when'll th' coffee be ready?" Coot Hendrick had apparently undergone a miraculous recovery.

"Hold your horses," said Mule, "it just started drippin'."

"You can git me a glass of tea, then, I wouldn't mind havin' a glass of tea."

"Coffee's all we got, take it or leave it."

"You don't have to bite my head off," said Coot. He coughed loudly to remind people that he'd been very sick, and that pneumonia was no laughing matter even if was the walking kind.

"Surprise!" yelled an arriving party-goer.

"It *ain't* a *su'prise,*" said Percy, who was tired of hearing that it was.

"How come?" asked Mule. "We told people not leak it to a livin' soul."

Velma, who had obviously spent the better part of the morning at Fancy Skinner's, peered over her glasses. "Blabbermouth Jenkins let th' cat out of th' bag."

"Why is this blasted coffeepot leaking water all over the burner?" asked Father Tim. "Mule! Can you step over here and take a look at this?"

"I'm cuttin' cake, buddyroe. Ask Percy."

"Percy's worked this counter for forty years. I'm giving him a break."

"Suit yourself, it's runnin' down on th' floor."

Blast! He flipped the switch to "off."

Ray Cunningham helped himself to a counter stool. "I hear coffee's on th' house! I'll have a little shooter, and one for your former mayor here."

"Ray, good to see you!" said Father Tim. "Esther, do you how to work this blasted coffeemaker?" Their former mayor could fix anything, including people's lives.

"Let me get back there," said Esther. "I'll handle this."

"Rev'ren', how you doin'?" Harley Welch's grin was wrapping clear around his head.

"Hey, buddy! Help yourself to a piece of cake. We're looking forward to having your feet under our table tomorrow."

"I've done made m' pan of brownies. I b'lieve they git better by settin' overnight."

"That seems to improve a good many things in life. Why, look here, it's Lew Boyd!"

"Father, meet Miz Earlene Boyd."

"Earlene!" Every head turned. He supposed he'd shouted.

"I'm glad to meet you, Father Tim."

"My goodness, Earlene, you're pretty as a picture."

"Who'd you say this is?" asked Coot Hendrick.

"My wife. Miz Earlene Boyd."

"Hey," said Earlene, shaking hands.

"His what?" asked an onlooker. "What'd he say?"

"His *wife*."

"His *wife?* I ain't believin' that! She's too good-lookin' to fool with him."

"From Tennessee," said Lew. He rocked back on his heels, about to bust the zipper off his jacket.

"Tennessee!" said Lois Holshouser. "I used to go out with a boy from Tennessee. His name was Junior something, dark hair, medium build, would you know him? I wouldn't mind lookin' him up."

Percy pumped Lew's hand with real feeling. "Congratulations!"

"I guess I'm too late t' claim my photo prize."

"You went an' got y'r own prize, looks like."

Earlene smiled at Father Tim. "Lew told me you know our circumstances. I appreciate you helpin' him."

"I'm not sure I've been any help, Earlene. But I must say we're happy to see you. To what do we owe this wonderful surprise?"

"Two days ago, Mama sat up in bed and looked at me like she knew who I was. An' you know what she said?"

"I'm eager to hear."

"She said, 'Earlene, I want you to be happy.'"

"Ah!"

"I nearly fell over, she'd never said anything like that. I said, 'Mama, can I tell you somethin'?' I just had this peace that it was right to say it—I said,

'Mama, I am happy, I'm married to a wonderful man.'

"All this time I thought she'd drop over with a heart attack an' everybody would blame me, but she just patted my arm." Tears pooled in Earlene's eyes.

"I said, 'Mama, do you mind if I run down to North Carolina for a little bit?' She said, 'No, honey, you go on, I want you to be happy.' Those were her exact words.

"So I got our neighbor to come in for five whole days."

"Five whole days!" said Lew.

"I get my retirement in nine months, and after that, I'll be movin' to Mitford. I'm so excited!"

"We'll be proud to have you," said Father Tim.

"Lew said I could bring Mama with me."

Lew's Adam's apple worked overtime. "We got an extra bedroom."

"I wanted my visit to be a surprise, so

when I got here yesterday evenin', I parked behind th' privet 'til Lew drove up. After he went in th' house, I stuck my head in th' door and hollered, 'Anybody home?' You nearly fell over, didn't you, baby? Father, do you like surprises?"

"I must tell you, Earlene, I'm not much on being surprised, but my wife is!"

New arrivals pushed through the door, driving early arrivals to the rear.

"Did I hear you're givin' your boy a *rototiller?*" Bob Hartley asked his boothmate.

"That's right."

"He's forty-two an' workin' a steady job. Why can't he buy 'is own ro-totiller?"

"We like to be nice to Harry; he'll choose our nursin' home."

Mitford's former mayor had the cof-feepot up and running and was pouring and serving as if she were campaigning for office. "Percy, you ol' coot, where'm I supposed to get a decent bowl of grits for breakfast?"

"Beats me," said Percy. "An' don't count on gettin' grits in Wesley, they're educated over there at th' college an' don't eat grits."

People were clearly happy to see their former mayor back in the thick of things, especially as their current mayor had been called to a social event at the governor's mansion.

"Congratulations, you dog!" Omer Cunningham, aviator, bon vivant, and in-law of former mayor Esther Cunningham, waded through the crowd, his big teeth gleaming like a piano keyboard. "Where are you an' Velma headed off to?" Omer gave Percy a slap on the back that nearly knocked him into the drink box.

"After gettin' up at four o'clock every mornin' for a hundred years, I'm headed off t' lay down an' sleep 'til Groundhog Day. Velma, she's headed off to th' pet shelter for a dadblame cat."

"Don't get a cat, get a dog!" someone urged.

"Don't get a dog, get a monkey!"

"Don't get nothin'," counseled the fire chief. "Animals strap you down—get somethin' with four legs an' you'll never see th' cherry blossoms, trust me."

Percy eyed the room—the booths and stools had filled up, and there was standing room only. Where were these turkeys when business had gone south a couple of times last summer?

"Speech! Speech!" someone hollered from the rear.

"Hold it!" J. C. Hogan blew in the front door, ushering a blast of arctic air into the assembly. "Make way for the press!"

"Oh, law!" whispered Minnie Lomax, who had closed the Irish Woolen Shop for this event. "It's J. C. Hogan—

he wants to be th' bride at every wed-
din' and th' corpse at every funeral."

A blinding flash went off, then another, and another.

"Stand over there with Velma," ordered the editor. "Velma, look here an'
give me a big grin! I know it's hard for
you to grin at me, but force yourself,
there you go, Betty Grable lives. Okay,
let's have a shot of Percy at th' grill.
Hey, Mule, move your big rear out of
this shot an' let Percy flip somethin' on
the grill. . . ."

"His last flip!" said Coot Hendrick.

Lois Holshouser wrinkled her nose.
"Who made this cake? Esther Bolick
didn't have anything to do with this
cake, I can tell you that right now."

"Store-bought," said Winnie Ivey
Kendall, who was not having any.

"Whose hat is this?" inquired Avis
Packard. "Somebody handed me this
hat. Is this your hat?"

"You're supposed to put somethin' in
it."

"Like what?"

"Money. For th' cherry blossoms."

"What cherry blossoms?"

Faye Tuttle announced a relative's sad news to Esther Cunningham. "Multiple dystrophy," said Faye, shaking her head.

J.C. mopped his brow with a paper napkin and handed off his Nikon to Lew Boyd. "Here you go, buddyroe, you won that big photo contest, crank off a shot of th' Turkey Club with Percy an' Velma. Come on, Mule, come on, Father, get over here. That's it, look right through there and push th' button. . . ."

Flash. Flash.

"Speech! Speech!"

Hand clapping, foot stomping. A spoon ringing against a coffee mug.

"I've made plenty of speeches th' last forty-four years," said Percy, "an' you've done forgot everything I said.

"So I ain't makin' a speech t'day except to say . . ."

In all his years as a regular, Father Tim had never seen Percy Mosely choke up. In case it was catching, he grabbed his handkerchief from his jacket pocket.

". . . except to say . . ."

"What'd he say?" asked someone in the rear.

". . . to say . . ."

"Looks like he can't say it."

It was catching, all right. Father Tim peered around and saw several people wiping their eyes. Velma pushed forward from the crowd. "What he's tryin' to say is, thanks for th' memories."

"Right!" said Percy, blowing his nose. Applause. Whistles.

"Great speech!" said Coot.

"You mustn't miss your nap," Cynthia reminded him.

They were slurping her Roasted Red

Pepper and Tomato Soup to a fare-thee-well. He could eat a potful of this stuff.

"I'll lie on the sofa when we finish the tree, and look at the lights. I'm sure I'll nod off."

"I think you should nap for at least an hour. But do you really want to lie on *that* sofa? Ugh! It's so Victorian, you can't possibly be comfortable."

"I'll get a pillow from the bed."

"I'll bring you one, and a blanket, too."

"Thanks. We've both been too blasted busy." *Slurp.* It was hard not to slurp soup. "But there's light at the end of the tunnel, my love!"

"Did you get through with you-know-what?"

"I did, by the skin of my teeth. And how about *your* you-know-what? The odor seeping from your workroom smells terrible. What's the deal?"

She laughed. "You'll see!" Leaning

her head to one side, she nailed him
with her cornflower-blue eyes. "You
know what I keep thinking about?"

"That you can think at all these days
is a marvel to me."

"Our trip to Ireland."

"Ah."

"We are going?"

"God willing, we *are* going!"

She beamed. "So is everything in order for the service tonight?"

"It is. I just need to step down to
church around five o'clock and see
how the greening party is coming
along." He pushed his chair back and
rose from the table. "Killer soup, my
dear!"

"Anything I can do to help?"

"Absolutely. At midnight, make sure
you're in the front pew where you usually sit when I celebrate."

"That's it?"

"That's it." He leaned down and took
her chin in his hand and kissed her, lingering. "I like to see your eyelashes go

up and down and the little stars come out of you."

It was a beautiful tree.

Over the years, he'd had white pine, cedar, blue spruce, and Fraser fir. Fraser fir was his favorite, by far, though he harbored a deep affection for cedar.

Neither he nor Cynthia had any special ornament collections, just the motley assortment that had come their way and escaped being smashed during their collective moves. But look at it! It was glorious, the best in years, and the colored lights were perfection; he was a sucker for colored lights.

The day had begun upside down, but God in His mercy had righted it, and he was a happy man. He lay back on the pillow, which was faintly scented with wisteria, pulled the blanket over him, and listened to his dog snoring under the wing chair. The smell in the room! That raw, green, living scent that the overcivilized got to relish only once a year. . . .

Closing his eyes, he inhaled the fragrance as if starved.

"Over yonder by th' fence post—how 'bout that 'un?"

"It's too bent on top. The star might fall off."

"How 'bout this 'un right here? We 'bout t' walk right into this 'un."

The smell of woods and winter pasture, the crunch of hoarfrost under their feet, the stinging cold on their faces, the feel of the sled rope in his hand, and Peggy with her head wrapped in a red kerchief . . .

"I like that one," he said, pointing.

"Yo' mama say don't point."

"How'm I supposed to show you where it's at?"

"Don't say 'where it's at,' say 'where it is.' Talk to me 'bout how to reco'nize it."

"See the one with the wide branches

at the bottom and the broom sage growing around it? Over by that ol' stump?"

"Oh, law, child, that cedar tree take two strong men t' chop down—we jus' a bony woman an' a baby boy."

"I'm *not a baby*." He stomped his foot to drive this truth home. Would she never stop calling him that?

"Oh, you right, I forgot you ain't a baby, an' don't stomp yo' foot at me, little man. You hear what I say?"

"Yes, ma'am."

"That's better. Pick yo'self another tree."

"But that's the best one of any. Besides, Mama likes a big tree."

"You right. She do."

"It would make her smile." That should do the trick; Peggy wanted as much as he did to make his mother smile.

Peggy shaded her eyes with her hand and squinted at the tree.

He pulled on Peggy's skirt. "Will Mama get well?" He'd been afraid to ask, afraid of the answer.

"She gettin' well ever' minute we stand here talkin'. Sure as you're born, she goin' to get well."

Peggy laid her hand on his shoulder; he could tell by the way she touched him that she was telling the truth.

"We'll get Rufe t' chop it, then. I'll see can I find 'im."

He looked up at the tall, slender woman whom he knew to be capable of anything. "We could prob'bly do it ourselves, Peggy . . . just you an' me."

"You know what you is?"

"What?" He was relieved that she didn't look angry with him.

"Th' mos' tryin'est little weasel I ever seen."

Peggy stumped ahead with the axe in her hand. Her dress and apron were the same color as the winter gold of the broomstraw, her kerchief a slash of crimson against the gray and leafless trees.

"Pick up yo' feet, then, let's see can we *do* this thing! Lord Jesus, you got t' help us, that ol' tree be a hun'erd foot tall!"

"Tall as a mountain!" he shouted into the stinging cold.

"High as th' sky!" whooped Peggy.

They had dragged the huge tree home on the sled, its greenness dark and intense in its passage through the winter woods. When Rufe made a stand for it and stood it in the parlor, he and Peggy were dismayed to see that it wasn't as high as the sky, after all; it reached only halfway up the parlor wall.

Days later, he still smelled the sharply resonant odor of the resin that smeared his hands and clothes; the scent was there even after his bath in the wash-tub on the night they trimmed the tree.

"Look at that boy eat fried chicken!" said Reverend Simon at their small Christmas Eve dinner. "You're making a proper Baptist out of him, Madelaine!"

His mother smiled. But his father did not.

When he came downstairs on Christmas morning, the tree was there, shining with colored bulbs and festooned with ornaments and tinsel. His father was wearing a smoking jacket, though he never smoked, and there were the presents waiting to be opened, and something hidden behind the davenport. . . .

When he placed the Babe in the manger, he saw what he'd desperately hoped for—the light returning to his mother's eyes, the light that shone like the star on top of the great and benevolent cedar.

"Merry Christmas!" he and his parents chorused in unison.

He raced at once to the sideboard and

brought the shepherds to the manger, displacing a cow and a donkey to give them a better view, while his father fetched from the bookcase the men who had journeyed so long to the star.

After the long month of waiting, the scene was complete.

Certainly he hadn't known it then, but the blue bicycle that he discovered behind the davenport had something of the wonder of the Child in it—it was yet another miraculous gift, mimicking the far greater Gift. He'd been beside himself with joy.

There was no way he could tell Tommy, of course—for what if Tommy hadn't gotten a bike, or anything at all?

"What is it, Timothy?" His mother sat in the blue-painted kitchen chair by the window, shucking oysters with Peggy.

"Tommy maybe didn't get nothing," he said, forlorn in spite of himself.

"Anything." His mother's voice was

tender; she reached for him and drew him close.

"Look here!" Peggy suddenly stood and peered through the window. "Look who's comin' up th' road!"

In the bright afternoon light of Christmas Day, Tommy Noles wobbled up their drive on two wheels of his own.

Tommy had a bike, and the light had returned to his mother's eyes.

Until he married Cynthia, it had been the single happiest Christmas of his life.

Between his nap and the trek to the church, more than an inch of snow had fallen, which would undoubtedly inspire the merry greening party in their labors.

But, alas, he found no greening party, merry or otherwise. He found instead that he must unlock the double front doors and let himself in. As the key turned, the bells began to toll.

Bong . . .

The moment he stepped into the narthex, he smelled the perfume of fresh pine and cedar, and the beeswax newly rubbed into the venerable oak pews.

Bong . . .

And there was the nave, lovely in the shadowed winter twilight, every nuance familiar to him, a kind of home; he bowed before the cross above the altar, his heart full. . . .

Bong . . .

The greening of the church was among his favorite traditions in Christendom; someone had worked hard and long this day!

Bong . . .

Every windowsill contained fresh greenery, and a candle to be lighted before the service . . . the nave would be packed with congregants, eager to hear once more the old love story. . . .

Bong . . .

Families would come together from

near and far, to savor this holy hour. And afterward, they would exclaim the glad greeting that, in earlier times, was never spoken until Advent ended and Christmas morning had at last arrived.

Call him a stick-in-the-mud, a dinosaur, a fusty throwback, but indeed, jumping into the fray the day after Halloween was akin to hitting, and holding, high C for a couple of months, while a bit of patience saved Christmas for Christmas morning and kept the holy days fresh and new.

He knelt and closed his eyes, inexpressibly thankful for quietude, and found his heart moved toward Dooley and Poo, Jessie and Kenny . . . indeed, toward all families who would be drawn together during this time.

"Almighty God, our heavenly Father . . ." He prayed aloud the words he had learned as a young curate, and never forgotten. ". . . who settest the solitary in families: We commend to thy continual care the homes in which thy people dwell. Put far from them, we beseech thee, every root of bitterness, the desire of vainglory, and the pride of life. Fill them with faith, virtue, knowledge, temperance, patience, godliness. Knit together in constant affection those who, in holy wedlock, have been made one flesh. Turn the hearts of the parents to the children, and the hearts of the children to the parents; and so enkindle fervent charity among us all, that we may evermore be kindly affectioned one to another; through Jesus Christ our Lord."

In the deep and expectant silence, he heard only the sound of his own breathing.

"Amen," he whispered.

The snow had stopped entirely; the snowplow operators could stay snug in their beds tonight, after all.

He unlocked the door of the Oxford and felt for the fourth switch on the plate. Deep within the large building, used originally as an in-town horse stable, the light came on in the back room and spilled through the open door.

His heart beat up—this was the day, the moment he'd worked and waited for. He moved quickly along the darkened aisle between the tables and chairs, the chests and sideboards.

Fred, Lord bless him, had offered to put the figures in boxes, enabling him to carry more pieces at once. That good fellow was his Christmas angel, if ever there was one.

He caught his breath sharply, and stood motionless at the door.

There were the boxes . . .

And there, on the table in the center of the room, was the stable, sheltering the Holy Family.

"Hark! The herald angels sing,
'Glory to the newborn King;

Peace on earth and mercy mild,
God and sinners reconciled!'"

"They're gearing up!" said Mamy
Phillips to her cat, Popeye.

Mamy, who lived in a small house
next to Lord's Chapel, couldn't imagine why people would want to go to
church in the middle of the night. She
did confess however, that as she became increasingly wakeful in her old
age, the midnight service was something to look forward to, as, however
faint it might be, she could hear the
singing.

"O little town of Bethlehem, how still we
see thee lie!
Above thy deep and dreamless sleep the
silent stars go by.
Yet in thy dark streets shineth the
everlasting Light;
The hopes and fears of all the years are
met in thee tonight.

*For Christ is born of Mary, and gathered
     all above,
While mortals sleep, the angels keep their
     watch of wondering love.
O morning stars together, proclaim the
     holy birth,
And praises sing to God the King,
And peace to men on earth."*

Mamy pulled the top window sash down an inch or two. Then, by cupping her hand around her right ear and holding her breath for long periods, she was able to catch every word that floated out upon the frozen air.

*"While shepherds watched their flocks by
     night,
All seated on the ground,
The angel of the Lord came down,
And glory shone around. . . ."*

When the congregants poured out into the night through the red doors, a fresh snow was swirling down in large, feathery flakes, anointing collars and hats, scarves and mittens. Two people put their heads back and stuck out their tongues and felt the soft, quick dissolve of the flakes.

"Merry Christmas, Father!"

"Merry Christmas, Esther, Gene! God bless you! And there's Hessie, merry Christmas to you, Hessie!"

"Why, Tom Bradshaw! Merry Christmas! What brings you back to the sticks?"

Laughter. Vaporizing breath. The incense of snuffed candles wafting on the air . . .

"Merry Christmas, Cynthia!"

"Merry Christmas, Hope, how lovely you look! And Scott, dear—merry Christmas!"

"They're goin' home, now," Mamy Phillips said to Popeye. "They've sung themselves out, I expect."

She was relieved, actually, for even with the sash down, it was a strain to try to hear every word through a stone wall and a hedge. Time and again, they'd invited her to attend services over there, but she was still thinking about it.

She locked the sash and went to the kitchen, where she crumbled saltines into a glass of milk. Then she set down a saucer of milk for Popeye, wondering if she would ever understand what all that church business was about, anyway.

They sat on the study sofa, catching their breath.

"I'm exhausted!" she said, taking his hand.

"Ditto. Thoroughly."

"Happiness is very demanding."

"Agreed!" Thank God for his robe and slippers. The craziness was past; Christmas had come!

She put her head on his shoulder. "The angel tree was one of the most wonderful things I've ever done. So many families came in for their bags of food . . . They say more people will sit down to Christmas dinner in Mitford and Wesley than ever before."

"Well done," he said, squeezing her hand. "I'm proud of you."

"Thanks. Everyone worked so hard. I'd like to do it again next year, and the next."

He kissed the top of her head.

"Did I tell you about the little girl who walked five miles to fetch the two bags of groceries for her family?"

"Tell me." He put his head back and closed his eyes, savoring the peace and privilege of nothing more to be done.

"There was no way on earth she could have carried them home, so I drove her; I can't tell you what terrible living conditions I saw. Timothy, if we were younger, I'd love for us to adopt."

"You may get your wish. Dooley is

thinking of changing his name to Kavanagh."

"Ahhh."

"I asked him to think about it a while
longer. It's a serious step."

"You're always wise, Timothy."

"Not always."

"When do you think you'll tell him
about the money from Miss Sadie?"

"I don't know. He'll be twenty-one
in February, that may be the time. Her
letter asks us not to tell him 'til he can
shoulder the responsibility."

"You'll know when. God will tell
you when."

He glanced at the clock above the
mantel. Good grief! "Shall we do it?"

"Let's!"

They bolted from the sofa and
sprinted along the hall. "Okay," he said
when they reached the lamp table.
"Stop and close your eyes. Promise not
to look."

"I promise!"

He took her by the hand and led her

to the door of the living room. Though he'd personally set out each of the figures and arranged them near the manger at the base of their tree, he saw it all with new and wondering eyes. It was the light, perhaps, richer and more radiant in the deep of night.

"Now," he said.

He had done it all in order to see her face, and, instantly, she made it all worthwhile. "Timothy," she whispered. "Oh!"

He put his arm around her waist and drew her to him.

"Merry Christmas," he said, shy and solemn.

"Oh," she said again. "I can't find words. . . ."

Barnabas trotted up the hall and stood by them, wagging his tail.

"Does this lovely crèche have anything to do with your long weeks at the Oxford?"

"It does."

Tears coursed along her cheeks. "Did

you in some way . . . that is, what did
you do, exactly?"

"I painted it."

"You *painted* it?"

"Fred helped. He stippled the sheep.
We fixed an ear here and there. And a
hand. He helped with the camel, too."

"The camel!"

"Back there. In the bushes, sort of."

She dropped to her hands and knees
and examined the little colony of shepherds and wise men and animals and the
reverent and amazed parents kneeling
by the Child. She held her hand up to
him, and he took it and knelt beside her.

"I can't believe my eyes, Timothy.
Everything, every creature, is so lovely,
so . . . real, somehow."

"I was plenty nervous about doing it,
about getting it right. After all, you're
the artist in the family."

She stared into each face. "I love this
angel! How did you decide on these
wonderful colors for her robe and
gown?"

"We looked in a book," he said, feeling like a schoolboy.

"And this dear old shepherd, with his lovely bald head . . ."

"Autobiographical!"

"But the eyes on this camel!" She hooted with laughter. "He looks up to something, don't you think?"

"That camel was the straw that nearly broke my back! We worked on the eyes, but, alas, what can I say? Fred and I are not Leonardos."

"This is so exciting! I'm discovering a whole other part of my husband."

He shrugged, speechless, thrilled to the core with her praise.

She rose on her knees and put her arms around his neck and looked at him, beaming. "You've found something fresh and wonderful in yourself; God has given you a brand-new gift."

"No, not a gift." He was blushing. "But He did help me do it. It was hard."

"I can't take it all in, I'll be crawling

around under here for days." She returned to her hands and knees; Barnabas trotted in and lay behind the
angel.

"One more visitor to the stable!" he
announced. "Where the deuce is Violet?"

"On top of the refrigerator. Leave
well enough alone."

The refrigerator! "I'm hungry as a
bear," he said. "I'll fix us something;
how about a bowl of cereal?"

"I can't wait another minute to give
you yours, Timothy. Then I'll fix us
both a bowl of cereal. Help me up!"

"Ah, but who will help me up?" His
knees creaked like the hinges of a loose
shutter.

"You can't look," she said, as he
hauled her to her feet.

"I promise." He loved it when someone had a secret thing to present, and
asked him not to look, and he had to
promise he wouldn't.

"By the way, the angel is glorious.

Was there only one to gaze down upon this wondrous assembly?"

He faced the tree and, as an extra precaution, shut his eyes. "There were two, but . . . I dropped the other one and broke it." He hated the thought even now.

He heard her slippers whisper across the hall and back again.

"Timothy . . ."

"Yes?"

"You said you broke the other angel?"

"Yes," he said, feeling oddly sad and repentant.

"Would this be it?" she asked.

He turned and saw the angel with the serene countenance and slender feet held close, and complete, in Cynthia's arms.

His breath went out of him.

"Your broken angel is made whole," she said.

Ten

*I*t was that time before sunrise that elderly people in the coves around Mitford still called "first light." Nothing at all could be seen of the sun; the winter sky and snow-covered mountains beneath were gray as stone.

At the town museum, Uncle Billy Watson shuffled along the dark hallway in his bathrobe, carrying the tray under his arm and thanking the Good Lord the paint had dried overnight. He would set out her Santy and mix up the pancake batter, and, in a little bit, go wake her up.

His heart was pounding with pure excitement. "Th' way my ticker's a-goin'," he muttered, "th' gover'-ment's gittin' its money's worth out of them pills."

He fumbled for the switch plate inside the door of the kitchen. As three hundred watts blazed into the room, he nearly jumped out of his skin.

"*Law help!*" he hollered, surprised by his wife, whom he'd thought still sleeping. She sat in her chair looking mad as a wet hen, her white, uncombed hair standing ever'whichaway.

"Rose!" he said, concealing the tray behind his back.

"What?"

"*I didn't know you was up!*" He'd decided to talk plenty loud this morning so she could understand every word. After all, it was Christmas.

She scowled, pulling together dark, heavy eyebrows that looked like two woolly worms. "Here it is daylight," she squawked, "and not hide nor hair of Santy!"

He'd seen her mad plenty of times, but this was one for the dadgum books. He wanted to run down the hall and jump out the window in his stocking feet.

"It's snowin' out!" He was going to keep the peace today if it killed him. "He'll be along directly!"

"Everybody knows Santy never comes after daylight!"

"Ever'body knows he don't come a'tall if you're settin' there f'r 'im t' stumble over!"

"I just sat down here, Bill Watson. I was hiding by the Kelvinator 'til a minute ago."

"I reckon he must've got a look at you somehow." Boys howdy, if that was a fact, ol' Santy had took off a-runnin', an' by now he'd made it to th' other side of th' mountain. He continued to hold the tray behind his back, though it made his arm tremble.

"What he's done is not show up at all, just like people have said all along. And after you poked a stick up the chimney and made that awful mess!"

Still facing his wife, he maneuvered to the table they'd started housekeeping with, the cherrywood table he'd made with his own hands all those years ago. He slid the tray onto the table without making a sound, then turned around and looked at it sitting there on the checked oilcloth with the red bow taped to a handle. Keeping his back to his wife, he slipped the envelope from his pocket and onto the tray.

"Law help, Rose, *looky here!*"

"What?"

"Here on th' table!" He yelled over his shoulder, hoarse as a frog, *"Hit's y'r Santy!"*

The tray was beauteous, it truly was, and the handle pull on each side was just the trick for picking it up and carrying it around. He hoped she wouldn't recognize the pulls under their coat of green paint.

"What is it?"

"Wellsir, I reckon hit's a tray f'r earbobs an' brooch pins an' whatnot, like you been a-needin'." He went to her, leaning on his cane and carrying the tray.

Her face lit up. "A jewelry tray! I vow I always wanted a jewelry tray!"

"Santy must've come while we was sleepin'." He stood by her chair, presenting the tray. His right hand shook, which made the bow jump around.

"Why, Bill Watson! It's real nice—I *declare* it is!"

"Ol' Santy done pretty good, I reckon." His heart was about to bust.

"What's that lying on it?"

"Y'r tray's got a letter with it, looks like."

Carefully, he stooped and placed the tray in her lap, and, for that moment, his arthritis didn't bother him at all.

As good as he could hear, his wife could see. She picked up the envelope and, squinting through secondhand glasses from the Lion's Club, examined the inscription.

She caught her breath.

"I'll make us a pancake," he said, swallowing hard.

But his feet wouldn't move. Instead, he watched his helpmeet of more than fifty years, she the rose and he the thorn, as tears of happiness streamed along her wrinkled cheeks.

She took the letter from the envelope, unfolded it, and read aloud, lingering over the words as if each were a gift in itself.

"'My . . . dear . . . little . . . sister . . .'"

As his wife sounded out the words, he discovered a wonderful thing—he wadn't jealous n' more, not even a whit.

"'You . . . please me . . . very much . . . with . . . your . . . fine reading, . . .'"

He wiped his eyes on his sleeve, ashamed that he'd ever harbored a bitter thought toward Willard Porter, and, right then and there, without speaking his petition aloud, asked the Good Lord to forgive him.

In the small house in the pines at the end of the road, the coffeemaker kicked on and brewed four cups of Wal-Mart's breakfast blend as Lew Boyd slept warm next to his wife. Beyond the window, snow swirled as in a miniature globe.

He gave a loud snort, which startled him awake, and looked about as if uncertain of his surroundings. Then he saw Earlene nestled into the crook of his right arm.

His heart flooded with a joy he hadn't known before, not even on their furtive honeymoon to Dollywood. He gazed at the streaks of gray in her chestnut hair, and the little lines at the corners of her eyes and mouth, and felt the love beat up in him, and the thanksgiving, and didn't mind that his arm had gone numb as a two-by-four—nossir, he wouldn't disturb this moment for anything.

He remembered last night, how they'd gone to church down at First Baptist, and how he could hardly believe he was standing next to her, singing his heart out and hearing her voice lift onto the high notes. The sound was almost more than he could bear and keep his eyes dry.

He'd been awful proud to introduce Earlene around, and he'd never seen such a swarm of flabbergasted people. Some hugged her neck right off the bat, and everybody said they were mighty happy for him. A few said they figured something was going on with those visits to his old aunt in Tennessee.

Afterward, they'd jumped over to Wesley for Chinese take-out, and come home and sat down to eat at the kitchen table like normal people. As far as he could recall, he'd mostly gobbled his dinner at the kitchen sink since Juanita passed.

Then they hauled the fake tree from the corner of the dining room where it had stood against the wall for seven years, mashing one side completely flat.

They set it in a stand by the front window and went after it like a house afire, weaving six strings of colored lights among the branches and decorating with everything they could find in the long-neglected boxes. As they did this, the flat side fluffed out—the plastic branches fell into place, one by one, until the tree looked good as new. He and Earlene stood there like little young 'uns and clapped their hands.

The very thought made him grin like a monkey, and he turned his head and nuzzled his wife's hair, and offered a silent prayer.

Thank you. . . .

He didn't know whether to say "Thank you, God" or "Thank you, Lord," or "Thank you, Father." Down at church, Preacher Sprouse said all three at one time or another, even "Yaweh." Harley Welch called Him "Lord an' Master," sometimes talkin' about Him as if He was standin' right there, and Father Tim prayed like him and God was old friends, kind of like, "Hey, buddy, how's it goin'?"

It was hard to think about something new, like what to call the Almighty. He hadn't exactly closed his mind in church, but he hadn't exactly paid attention, either; he'd been bad to think about business when sitting in the pew—was gasoline goin' up or was it goin' down? Why couldn't this country find its own instead of leanin' on the Middle East? And why were customers so dadblame hard to please?

Then there was the EPA—the worst torment a man could have in this life. Forget down yonder, they made it hell enough right here! Every ten years, regular as clockwork, they checked him out, and ten years ago, they'd tore up his tanks and jackhammered his concrete pads an' dug down t' Beijing, an' th' mess they found had cost him thirty thousand smackers.

He thought he'd just let th' whole dadgum thing go south, but he'd tightened his belt and held on for everything he was worth, and somehow he'd made it through. Others hadn't been so lucky; he'd watched the EPA shut down his competition 'til he was the only gas station left open for eight miles to th' north an' six to th' south. Trouble was, in just three months, his ten years were up, and they'd be knockin' on his door again.

He felt his temples pounding just *thinkin'* about the gover'ment. . . . Nossir, he didn't want to do that, his blood pressure would shoot out th' roof, wake up Earlene, and set th' neighbor's dogs to barkin'.

He guessed th' only time he really paid attention in church was when it was time to sing. He'd heard enough preachin' to know that pride goeth before a fall, and he was prideful about his voice, he admitted it. As he was th' only bass at First Baptist, his singin' stood out, causing people to turn their heads and look, and sometimes even smile or give him a thumbs-up.

But th' bottom line was, he hadn't done right by God. Or th' Lord. Or th' Heavenly Father. Not that he'd killed anybody or coveted anybody's wife or anything like that, but, all his life, he'd gone on his merry way, doin' his own thing. To tell th' truth, he'd like to give it all to somebody bigger an' smarter than him.

One of these days, maybe he would pray that other prayer, after all. Something deep inside had shifted in a way he couldn't explain. He couldn't remember all the words Father Kavanagh had said, except the part about surrendering his life. That didn't seem so frightening now, with Earlene lying beside him and the snow brushing against the window and piling up on the railing outside.

He just couldn't imagine what possible interest Almighty God could have in his life . . . but . . .

He lay still for a long time, scarcely breathing, before finishing that thought.

. . . but if He wanted it, He could have it.

Hope stood at the windows looking down on Main Street. In truth, one could hardly tell there was a street there at all. The tracks of the snowplow, made less than an hour ago, were vanishing under fresh snow.

"Thank you, Lord!" she whispered, glad for the beauty and peace of this morning.

Since she had prayed that prayer last September, a lot of things had changed. It was easier and easier to blurt something out to God, or ask Him for guidance, or, right on the spot, thank Him for the simplest things.

The midnight service at Lord's Chapel had been transporting; she had never attended such a service. The smell of the cedar and pine . . . the lovely and moving voices of the choir, often singing a cappella in the candlelit church . . . and her hand warm in Scott's hand . . .

She knew she had never done anything to deserve any of this, which made God's love for her all the more amazing and inexplicable.

Walking toward the hot plate where she would soon prepare her first Christmas breakfast for company, she recognized the deep fatigue she felt from the long weeks of not knowing, and the lack of help with the rare-books business, and the loss . . . But it was Christmas, and she mustn't think of loss.

She felt compelled to turn and look at the light spilling through the lace.

"Mother!"

The grief was sharp and sudden, and

she put her head in her hands and wept, feeling, even in her sorrow, an assurance she could not define.

"We need a carrot!"

"We ain't got any carrots, I looked!"

"Dooley says don't say 'ain't'!"

"We could use a stick for 'is nose. I guess there's plenty of sticks around."

"Yeah, but how can you see where they're at under th' snow?"

In the yard of the small house in the laurels, Poo and Jessie Barlowe built a snowman that they planned to top off with their stepfather's yellow hard hat. Dooley would come over today, and they would go with him to the preacher's house for Christmas dinner, where they'd see their other brother, Sammy, and get presents. Then, maybe everybody would drive by their house and see their snowman. This possibility was so exciting they couldn't eat breakfast, though each had ventured out into the cold and snowy morning with a pocketful of M&M's.

"How can we make 'im smile?"

"Little rocks, like from a driveway. We could stick 'em in 'is face in a little curve."

"We don't have no driveway."

Jessie thought hard, her breath clouding the air in short puffs. "We could use M&M's!"

"I ain't usin' mine."

"I can't believe how selfish you are! Don't you know it's Christmas? Plus everybody might ride over to see."

"OK," said Poo, emptying his pocket.

She had never made an omelet using a two-burner hot plate, but Scott cheered her on, and with the salsa and toast and plum jam and tea, it all seemed magical. Sitting in her new home with Scott, his dogs sleeping on the old rug she loved, she felt suddenly grown-up and invincible, taller, even.

"Merry Christmas!" she said, overcome by his presence across her small table.

"Merry Christmas," he said, taking her hand.

She'd certainly had dreams of romance, sometimes even foolish dreams about men on moors, usually on horseback, with their capes blown by some stern highland wind. But never had she dreamed she might know someone so peaceable and kind, so genuine and true. She pressed his hand, unable to speak, and again felt tears shining in her eyes.

He settled back in the chair, looking easy and relaxed. "Tell me—what is your chief desire for Happy Endings?"

She thought for a moment. "I'd like my bookstore to be a place where people feel truly at home."

He smiled. "Your bookstore."

"Yes!" she said, marveling. "My bookstore!"

"You know what?"

"What?"

"Your bookstore is living up to its name."

It felt wonderful to laugh, as if the sound were coming from a new person, someone she was excited about getting to know. The dogs jumped up and ran to her at once, as if called by her laughter.

She looked into their brown and eager eyes. "May I give them a bite of toast with jam?"

"They'd like that."

She felt their soft, nuzzling way of taking the toast from her hand.

"Beautiful!" Scott said, with special tenderness. "Sparkling!"

She touched the small diamonds at her ears. "They're wonderful, I love them!"

He grinned. "I wasn't talking about the earrings," he said.

On the deck of Esther and Gene Bolick's green cottage east of Main Street, fourteen terra-cotta flowerpots filled with snow, and mounded like ice cream cones.

Beyond the sliding doors, Esther and Gene sat by the fireplace in their twin recliners, drinking coffee and opening presents. The fake fireplace, which Gene had given her ten Christmases ago, featured a forty-watt bulb that glowed through a revolving sheet of red cellophane, a setup that Esther had often pronounced "cozy."

"I can't *believe* this!" said Esther.

"What?" Gene had just opened a can of nuts from a pal at the Legion hut, and was searching for a cashew.

"This laundry bag with the *B* monogram! From Hessie Mayhew!"

"What about it?"

Incredulous, Esther held the gift aloft. "I put this old thing in th' Bane an' Blessin' a hundred years ago!"

"Well, I'll be," said Gene, trying to sound interested.

Esther dropped the laundry bag into

her lap and sat frozen with disbelief. "And to think I gave her a *two-layer marmalade*."

"Th' poor woman has a gimp leg, Esther, which don't leave much room for shoppin'. Besides, why did you put it in th' Bane an' Blessin'? It looks perfectly good to me."

"Well, yes," said Esther, examining it more carefully. "After I put it in, I wished I hadn't."

"See?" said her husband, hammering down on a couple of cashews. "What goes around comes around."

At Hope House, Louella Baxter Marshall rolled onto her right side, heaved herself up, and sat on the edge of the bed.

"Merry Christmas, Miss Sadie! Merry Christmas, Moses, honey. Merry Christmas, my sweet boy in heaven! Merry Christmas, Mama!"

A string of lights twinkled on a red

poinsettia on her windowsill; thirty-two Christmas cards were Scotch-taped to her doorframe. It was a nice Christmas, yes, it was, and, about three o'clock, she would put on her new cherry lipstick and a dab of eye shadow in a color that looked good with her skin, and the nurse would help zip her blue dress with the long sleeves. Then she would wrap the little something she'd bought for Father Tim and Miss Cynthia, who were nearly as close as kinfolk, and her little preacher, Scott Murphy, would carry her off to the Kavanaghs' for a fine dinner.

"Miss Louella, are you talkin' to yourself this mornin'?"

"I'm wakin' myself up. Merry Christmas!"

"Merry Christmas to you! We got a big snow in th' night, and it's still comin'."

Louella did not care for snow, and refused to recognize this observation.

"Are you ready for a nice breakfast this mornin'?"

"What is it, honey?" She knew they tried hard, but she didn't think much of the victuals at Miss Sadie's rest home.

"It's turkey sausage with scrambled eggs, and one of your nice biscuits."

"You take th' sausage on back an' leave me th' biscuit an' eggs." Sausage from a turkey! What was the world comin' to? "An' when you step down to Miss Pattie's room, would you carry this?"

Louella placed a small gift, tied with a red ribbon, on the tray. "I ain't got but one visit in my bones t'day."

"Yes, ma'am, Miss Louella."

"An' don't let me go off an' forget my pan of rolls from th' kitchen."

"No, ma'am, I won't. You want this little string of lights turned off?"

"No, I don't. I want it left on 'til Christmas is over."

"That would be tomorrow," said

Nurse Austin, who hated to see electricity wasted in broad daylight.

"No, honey, Christmas ain' over 'til midnight on January six."

"Is that right!" said Nurse Austin, who was accustomed to residents with memory problems and general confusion.

One mile north of the Mitford monument, Old Man Mueller sat at his breakfast table in the unpainted house surrounded by a cornfield, and, with his dentures soaking in a jar by the bed, devoured a large portion of the cake Esther and Gene Bolick had brought him last night on Christmas Eve.

He didn't have any idea why they would bring him a cake every Christmas, as he hardly knew them or anybody else at that rock church on Main Street. All he knew is, if one year they forgot and didn't show up, he'd set down and bawl like a baby.

His dog, Luther, who was known to have a total of 241 separate freckles on his belly, stood and placed his paws on the table, gazing solemnly at his master.

"Don't be givin' me th' mournful eye," said Old Man Mueller. He dragged the cake box over, cut a good-size piece, slapped it into an aluminum cake pan, and set the pan on the floor.

"There!" he said. "An' Merry Christmas to y'r brute self."

"Bill Watson!"

"That's m' name, don't you know."

"You're the best ol' Santy ever was."

"*I ain't no Santy!* What makes you think such as that?"

"I have two eyes in my head, and a brain!"

He had no idea what to reply to such a statement.

In her slippers and robe, Miss Rose shuffled to the chair by the window where he sat with his cane between his knees, watching the snow top off the monument.

She leaned down and laid her head on his, and put her arms around his neck. "You've always been my good ol' Santy," she said.

He patted her bony arm with an inexpressible happiness.

"An' always will be," he replied. "Always will be."

In the study of the yellow house on Wisteria Lane, an e-mail rolled into Father Tim's mailbox.

<Emma Catherine Grayson

<8 lbs 9 oz

<4 o'clock this morning.

<All well.

<Merry Christmas and hallelujah!

<Love, Emma

Even on this gray, snowbound morning, the dining table in the yellow house looked festive and expectant. Sitting on a heavy linen cloth were a low vase of yellow roses and a ham platter decorated with exotic birds, which Cynthia had found in a long-ago ramble through New England. On the sideboard, the Kavanagh family silver gleamed in a shaft of early light.

Father Tim was awake, as was his wife, though they hadn't climbed into bed until after three o'clock.

"I thought I'd never go to sleep," said Cynthia.

"It was the excitement," said Father Tim.

"Plus the caffeine! I drank coffee yesterday afternoon with the Methodists. Will I never learn?"

He yawned. "Wait 'til we get some Irish coffee in you."

"Who do you think it was, Timothy?"

"Who what was?"

"The stable. Who do you think did it?"

"I don't know. I almost don't want to know."

They lay together, happy and exhausted, like two spoons in a drawer.

"It's all a miracle," she whispered.

"Yes!" he said. "To think that you'd come to take me to lunch just after Fred carried the box with the broken angel to the alley! Truth really is stranger than fiction."

She had her go at yawning. "I parked behind the Oxford and walked up the alley and, nosey me, looked into that box sitting on the garbage can. When I saw her lovely face, I knew at once I wanted her. I'd worked with plaster years ago, and believed I could make her whole.

"I brought it home and thought, Timothy gave Hélène his beautiful bronze angel, I want to do this for him. Because if I could do it, it would represent the very reason Christ was born. He came to put us back together, and make us whole."

"Christmas is real," he said. "It's all true."

"Yes," she said. "It's all true.

"Merry Christmas, my love."

"Merry Christmas, dearest."

"By the way," he said. "What was that noxious smell coming from your workroom?"

"Auto body putty! The perfect solution for putting together all those smashed pieces."

She snuggled her head into the crook of his arm. "You know, Timothy— since the table is set and most of the cooking is done, and since we got to bed so late and it's still so early, and since no one is coming until four, and since I hardly *ever* get to do it . . ."

"Spit it out, Kavanagh."

". . . I'm going back to sleep!"

"Wonderful idea! And since Barnabas went out at two-thirty, and since the ham is glazed and the fire is laid and the egg nog is done and the front steps are salted, I'll join you!"

He punched up his pillow and pulled the covers to their chins, and held his wife closer.

After all, it was Christmas.

"And the child grew, and waxed strong in spirit, filled with wisdom: and the grace of God was upon him."

Luke 2:40, KJV

LIKE WHAT YOU'VE SEEN?

If you enjoyed this large print edition of **Shepherd's Abiding**, here are a few of Jan Karon's latest bestsellers available in large print.

In This Mountain (trade paperback)
0-375-72820-1 (($14.95/$22.95C)

A Common Life (trade paperback)
0-375-72814-7 (($12.95/$19.95C)

Large print books are available wherever books are sold and at many local libraries.

All prices are subject to change. Check with your local retailer for current pricing and availability. For more information on these and other large print titles visit www.randomhouse.com/large print.